Love ya Babe

Love ya Babe

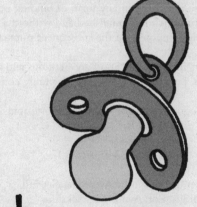

Chris Higgins

*Hodder
Children's
Books*

A division of Hachette Children's Books

For my family, as always. Love ya babes!

Thanks Lily.

Today I found an abandoned baby on the tube.

I was on my way back from Oxford Street with Angie. We'd gone up after school to see the lights and do a spot of late-night Christmas shopping. As far as our mums were concerned we'd stayed late at school, practising for the carol concert. I can't sing for toffee but I do play the violin (badly, considering the millions of lessons I've had) and because there are only two of us at our school who do, and the other one is the music teacher, I'm in demand at this time of year. Angie's got a lovely voice, sweet and clear as a bell, and she always gets to sing the solo, so both our mums believed us when we said we had a rehearsal.

We'd bought lots of small stuff like jewellery and make-up and underwear with Christmas motifs on them so we could get them home without anyone noticing. We're busy sifting through them when this dead fit boy gets on and sits down next to me. I pull a pair of bright red knickers covered in sprigs of holly out of my pocket and pretend to examine them to see what he'll do. Angie starts to giggle. She gets up and stands with her back against the pole, her phone out ready to take a photo, but he's got his ears plugged into his iPod and his face stuck inside a free newspaper and he doesn't bat an eyelid. After a while she turns her attention elsewhere.

'Aahh,' she says. 'Aren't you gorgeous?'

'What?' I lift my head, startled. I'd stuffed the knickers back in my pocket so I could inspect the five pairs of earrings I'd bought: one for Mum, one for Grandma, one for Angie (she'd chosen them but she still wanted them wrapped up), one for me for going out, one for my brother Felix (no, I'm joking), one spare in case someone bought me a surprise Christmas present. Well, you never know, do you? They'd got tangled up together in the bag and I was trying to sort them out.

'Look, Gabs,' she says. 'Blooming beautiful, yeah?'

Angie was bending over, her head inside a pram. Might've known it. Angie's attracted to babies like magnets are to fridge doors. You'd think she'd have had enough with all the kids in her family: she's got so many, all of them living in the same block of flats, you can't tell who's a proper sibling, who's a step, who's a cousin and who's just wandered in off the street. It's the same with the grown-ups, everyone's called Aunty or Uncle Something though I'm sure they're not all related. For ages, when I first got to know her, I thought her gran was her mum.

It's not surprising really. She calls her Mimi, everyone does. Plus, her gran looks loads younger than *my* mum.

'Yeah,' I agree, trying not to sound as bored as I felt. Honestly, Angie's hopeless. Last summer we went down to Brighton for the day on the train on our own and we walked along the seafront to eye up the talent but I swear she was far more interested in inspecting the contents of the baby buggies. She'll end up like her mum, with a baby at sixteen, the way she's going.

'Come and have a look, Gabs.' She's practically drooling over this pram. Its hood is up but she's pushed her face up close and is grinning inanely at the contents. I sigh, put away the earrings and stand up obediently. Angie moves back to let me see. Two dark eyes stare up at me from inside a nest of blankets. It's a little girl, ebony-skinned, a curl of jet-black hair caught up in a red festive ribbon on top of her head.

'Cute,' I say perfunctorily, but to be honest I'm not that impressed. I don't really get babies. From the little I know about them, they seem to be a whole lot of hard work for no gain. As far as I can remember from my little brother Freddie who's six now, going on seven, they cry a lot, are sick all the time, do horrible stinky things in their nappies and keep everyone awake at night. Like, why would you go gaga over someone with no teeth who can't even control their own bowel movements? I mean, we'd been to the old people's home to do a Christmas concert last week and I didn't see Angie simpering all over the old biddies there. It's the same thing, isn't it?

Suddenly I sneeze, twice. Loudly. It's hard to sneeze silently. It's *impossible* to sneeze with your eyes open, I've tried it.

'Ahh, you made her laugh!'

I look back at the pram. For some reason the baby seems to think my sneezing is outrageously funny. She's smiling up at me in delight, her cheeks stretched wide in a big gummy grin. I laugh and she chuckles back at me, her eyes shining.

'She thinks you're hilarious, Gabby!'

'I am, aren't I?'

To my surprise, she coos back at me. I've never spoken directly to a baby before, not since I've grown up I mean. I always thought they wouldn't know what you were talking about and I'd feel stupid. And there was no way I'd ever do that baby talk thing in a high, squeaky voice, it's too embarrassing. Anyway, I've never actually come across a baby at such close quarters before, not since

Freddie, which was ages ago. As far as I can remember, I used to avoid him as much as possible, like I do now.

The baby sounds just like one of the pigeons in Trafalgar Square. I giggle and say without thinking, 'You're a little birdy, you are,' and then I feel silly because I've used baby language after all, but she chuckles again as if she thinks that's the funniest thing she's ever heard. I'm right, she *is* cute.

I straighten up and her smile disappears. She studies me intently as is if she's afraid she'll miss something, like I'm a stand-up comic and she's my number one fan. Her eyes are wide open and framed by long, dark lashes. She's waiting. 'What?' I ask her. 'What do you want?'

She beams again and arches her back in delight, pushing her tummy up.

Angie laughs. 'I never knew you were good with babies.'

'I'm not! I don't like them.'

'She likes you!'

It's true, she does. I cross my eyes and she chortles and waves her arms about. She gives a little grunt as if she's prompting me to entertain her some more so I cross my eyes again, sticking my tongue out as well this time for good measure. I'm rewarded with a series of chuckles from the pram, like she's having a convulsion or something. IPod Boy gets up and stands by the door, like he thinks it's a good idea to make a quick getaway. I stick my tongue out at *him* this time, behind his back.

'Who does she belong to?' asks Angie.

'Dunno.' I glance around. 'Those two, I guess.'

I indicate a couple talking animatedly. The baby's eyes move from my face to Angie's and back and she grunts again, seeking my attention. She likes me best. The train slows down as it pulls into a station and the doors open. IPod Boy quickly steps down on to the platform followed by nearly everybody else in the carriage, including the couple who dive off at the last minute.

'Oops! They've forgotten her!' I say and Angie looks momentarily stunned as the doors close and the train pulls away. 'Only joking!'

'Who's she with then?'

I glance around and spot a blonde woman sitting further down the carriage, reading to a toddler on her knee. 'Her, I suppose.'

Angie snorts. 'I don't think so.'

'Why not?'

'Duh!' She grins at me, showing her even, white teeth. 'Wrong colour?'

'Oh yeah.' I grin back. The baby could have been Angie's actually, she's got the same perfect dusky skin and bright eyes. She's still staring unblinkingly at me, like I'm the most fascinating person she's ever seen in her life,

6

then, suddenly, she gives a huge, pink yawn, her mouth so wide she looks as if she's going to swallow herself. Her fists come up to scrub furiously at her eyes then she turns her head to one side, puts her thumb in her mouth, encircles her nose with a tiny finger and clutches compulsively at the top of her blanket with her other hand. Her eyes close. Within seconds she's fast asleep. I feel disappointed. No, more than that, I feel dismissed, like when I've had a telling-off at school and it's all over and I'm told to go. My presence is no longer required.

'She's got to be with someone,' insists Angie.

I look up and down the carriage. There's a bloke asleep on his own, his head lolling back, mouth open, the shadow of fatigue beneath his eyes. A rucksack lies at his feet. He looks as if he's on his way home from work. 'Can't be him.'

'What about her then?' Angie nods towards an old woman with untidy grey hair, surrounded by bags. She's bundled up inside woolly cardigans, a grubby scarf and a big scruffy coat and she's mumbling away to herself.

'No way!' My lip curls in derision. My eyes move back to the sleeping baby, clean and well-cared-for in her nest of soft blankets, even if her pram isn't brand-new. Somebody loves her and it's definitely not some old bag lady. I search the carriage again. The only other occupants left are two boys in school uniform, flicking bits of paper at each other, and an elderly Chinese couple. 'Do you think she's with them?'

It was Angie's turn to be scathing. 'Like, on a scale of one to ten, I guess that's a nought.'

'Well, there's nobody else.'

'Do you think she's been abandoned?' Angie's face lights up with excitement. She loves a drama, does Angie.

'Don't be daft,' I say automatically. 'She can't have been.'

But my voice falters. Could she? Could someone abandon a little scrap like that? Maybe. You read about stuff like this in the newspaper every day. I glance up at the tube map. 'It's our stop next.'

'What are we going to do?' asks Angie, looking genuinely upset. 'Poor little thing. We can't leave her here.'

'She's got to be with someone.'

'Who? Gabby, we get off in a minute!'

'I don't know! Let me think.'

'I bet it was that couple. I bet they've got no money to look after her. Maybe he's found out she's not his and he's given his girlfriend an ultimatum. Me or the baby, but you can't have us both. Or maybe they've kidnapped her and now they've got the ransom, they're ditching her. I bet they're—'

'Angie, SHUT UP!' The train's slowing down. The sleeping guy wakes up, stretches and picks up his bag. The woman closes the book and sets the toddler on her feet, holding her steady by the arm as the train lurches its way into the station. The bag lady continues arguing with herself and the Chinese couple stare impassively out of the window as the platform appears. The boys stand up, slinging their bags on their shoulders and move towards the door, tripping each other up as they go. There's a gasp of brakes as the train comes to a halt and the doors swish open.

'What are we going to do!' Angie's face is pleading, urgent.

'I don't know!'

'Right! I'm going to find someone, quick. You get the pram off, I'll get a guard.'

Angie leaps off the train and disappears up the platform. The boys and the man follow and I wait for the woman with the toddler to alight. I'm going to have to manhandle the pram on to the platform on my own, somehow.

'Excuse me.'

'Sorry?'

'Excuse me. Can I get to my pram?'

'Is she yours?'

'Yes.'

'She can't be.' My hand curls protectively round the handle.

The woman gapes at me in surprise. 'I beg your pardon?'

I study her and her little girl, both of them blonde and pink-cheeked.

I look at the sleeping baby, black hair with red bow, dark-skinned. Perfect.

'She's . . . different.'

'What?' She's irritable. 'Look I need to get off here.' She puts out her hand to reach for the pram and automatically my grip tightens. At that moment, Angie reappears, panting and red-faced, with an official in tow, a big burly guy in uniform wearing a bright yellow, day-glo safety jacket.

'What's going on here?' he asks.

'I'm trying to get off the train,' says the woman icily. 'This girl is obstructing me.'

The official glowers at me.

'It's not her baby!' I say desperately. 'It can't be.'

The man turns to her. 'Is this your baby, madam?'

'Yes. Well, no actually. Not exactly.'

'See!' I say triumphantly. 'She's trying to steal it!'

'Of course, I'm not! Don't be ridiculous.' The woman turns on me ferociously. 'I'm her child-minder, for goodness sake.' She forages around in her bag and brandishes a card at us triumphantly. 'Look! Here's my ID. I've been checked by the county council, you know!'

My heart sinks.

'We need to check this out,' says the official. 'Off the train, please! Come with me, all of you.'

'For goodness sake!' snaps the woman, shooting me a look of pure venom. 'I'm going to be late now! Her mother will be worried sick!'

Angie looks round wildly as if she's contemplating making a run for it. The official must have thought so too because he grabs her by the arm. 'Not so fast, young lady,' he says and the next second he's calling for assistance on his radio mike. Within minutes we're all being escorted to the lift by more day-glo, luminescent look-alikes.

'My gran'll go crazy if I'm arrested!' whispers Angie.

'It's all your fault!'

'No it isn't!'

'I'm sorry,' I plead miserably to the woman's back, ramrod straight with rage, as she blazes along the platform, pushing the pram before her. 'It was all a mistake!'

In answer she turns round and stabs me furiously through the heart with her eyes. I fall silent, wounded to the core. The baby wakes up and starts crying.

Honestly, it could only happen to Angie and me. It *was* her fault.

I don't even like babies, for goodness sake!

It works out all right in the end, after we explain everything to the transport police. Poor Angie, she was trembling. She was scared stiff her gran would find out. Mimi is pretty fearsome; she rules the whole family with a rod of iron, and she'd go absolutely ballistic if Angie was to get in trouble with the police.

I don't want my mother to find out either but for a different reason. Mum would never let me hear the end of it. She'd be telling the story at yoga-lunches and parents' evenings for years to come. She doesn't actually have a life of her own, even though she clogs it up with as many pointless activities as she can. Instead she lives vicariously through her children and seems to expect everyone else to find us as fascinating as she does.

They don't.

Actually, I'm not too keen on my dad finding out either. Not the way he is at the moment.

Anyway, it didn't come to that, thank goodness. The woman calmed down eventually, once they'd checked her credentials. In the end she even seemed to see the funny side of it. We were free to go.

When we get outside the station, Angie races off because she'll get it in the neck for being late. I debate getting a taxi but then remember I've spent all my money in the shops. Anyway, I won't get in trouble like Angie, just as long as I'm home before Dad. Mum'll have her hands full with Freddie and won't even have noticed I'm late. So I set off walking in the other direction. You'd never think we were in the same catchment area for our school. Angie lives in the flats on the estate. I live in one of the so-called posh houses by the park.

By the time I get home, I'm starving.

'What's for tea?' I yell as soon as I get through the door. All the low-energy lights in our house are blazing furiously. That's my mother, a walking, talking, contradiction in terms. She's for ever reading up about how we should be saving the planet and spends a fortune on being green.

The house is nice and tidy, the cleaner's been. From upstairs I can hear water splashing and somebody screaming blue murder. (What is blue murder, by the way? As opposed to ordinary murder, that is.)

'Where've you been?'

My brother, Felix, is huddled under a duvet on the sofa watching television. He's wearing an Alice band.

'That's mine,' I say automatically.

'No it's not, I bought it myself.'

'Don't let Dad see you wearing it.'

He pulls a face.

'How was school?'

He pulls a worse face and snuggles further under the duvet. 'Why are you late?'

'Been shopping. Got your Christmas pressie.'

His face lights up. 'Can I see it?'

I empty the earrings on to the sofa. 'Take your pick.'

He looks up at me quizzically. 'Are you serious?'

'Get real! What do you want, anyway?'

His face falls. 'Dunno. I'll have a think.'

'Where's Mum?'

'Bathing Freddie. Can't you hear?'

Freddie's wails pierce the air. Even for him, they're impressive.

'He's having his hair washed.'

'He's nearly seven. He should be washing his own hair,' I say irritably, scooping the earrings back into my pocket. 'Angie's little sister's not even five and she can shower and wash her own hair.'

'Freddie can't even wipe his own bum,' observes Felix.

Then he adds in a touching moment of honesty, 'He can beat me at footie though.'

'And tag rugby, and swimming, and cricket, and running,' I point out helpfully.

'And catching, and short tennis. Most things really,' Felix says morosely. 'Horrible little beast.'

'Never mind. He still acts like a baby half the time.'

'I know.' Felix brightens up. 'Mum was feeding him at teatime, off a spoon, because he wouldn't eat his tea. She made a potato mountain for him with a fish finger fort at the top. She said the peas were enemy soldiers going up the mountain and every time he ate one, he'd captured a soldier.'

'Did it work?'

'Yep. He scoffed the lot. He would've done anyway. He was just attention-seeking.'

'He'll want her to do that all the time now. He's so spoilt.'

I go into the kitchen to find something to eat. There's a smell of burning. Something veggie, grainy and disgusting is bubbling dry on the stove. I wish I'd come home earlier and had a fish finger fort for tea. I turn the heat down and give it a stir, mixing in the black bits stuck to the bottom of the pan, then I help myself to one of Mum's organic, wholemeal scones (home-made of course) plastering it in 'locally-sourced' honey. Yeah, like there are millions of beehives round here. Upstairs the yells subside. I can hear Mum's voice singing a song I remember from my bedtimes in the dim and distant past. I pour myself a glass of milk and smother another scone with honey.

'Here she is! Here's your big sister.' Mum comes into the kitchen, out of breath, with Freddie in her arms. His legs are trailing practically all the way down to the floor. He's far too big to be carried. 'Look at this nice clean boy.'

I eye Freddie with distaste. He's blond-haired and blue-eyed which means he should be appealing, all pink-cheeked and smelling of soap as he is from his hot bath. But my little brother, far from being irresistible, is very resistible indeed, because, along with his clean, well-pressed pyjamas he's wearing his usual grumpy frown and the downturned mouth he's inherited from Dad, and he's sniffing unbecomingly.

'What's up with him?'

'He doesn't like the nasty water going in his eyes, do you, darling?' says Mum, cuddling him to her.

'He swims for his school, for goodness sake. He should be used to water in his eyes.'

'Not with nasty, stingy shampoo in it,' says Mum, nuzzling his neck. Freddie twists away from her attentions and she staggers slightly as his not

16

inconsiderable weight is dispersed in her arms.

'Put him down, for goodness sake, you'll drop him,' I say, turning away in disgust.

Mum thankfully places him on the floor. 'He's getting to be such a big boy, aren't you, darling?'

'Yes, he's seven soon,' I say cuttingly, but it's wasted on Mum.

'My baby,' she coos and pulls him back towards her for a cuddle. Squashed against her not inconsiderable stomach and unseen by her, he sticks his tongue out at me. I pull a face in return. Freddie whines.

'Don't do that, darling,' says Mum, her arms closing protectively around him. 'It frightens him.'

'Stop babying him. He's a monster.'

She's not listening. She never does. She hasn't even noticed I'm late home.

Yes she has.

'You've missed tea, Gabby, so you can have supper tonight with Mummy and Daddy when Daddy gets home.'

'Yippee.'

The sarcasm's lost on her. She's too busy brushing Freddie's hair up into blond peaks. He looks ridiculous.

'*I* want supper with Mummy and Daddy,' whines Freddie.

'Freddie needs his sleep,' says Mum. 'It's Freddie's

bedtime and Mummy's going to read him a lovely story.'

'I don't want a story!' yells Freddie. 'I want to watch television.'

I don't blame him either. Mum's idea of a bedtime story is disgustingly twee. She's the master (or should I say the mistress) of the silly voice and she likes to get into the persona of all the different characters. It's so annoying.

'It's too late for television, sweetheart. There are only grown-up, scary programmes on now.'

'I like grown-up, scary programmes!'

'They'll give Freddie bad dreams.'

'Felix is watching it!'

'Felix is four years older than you!' I retort furiously.

'Turn it off, Felix darling,' calls Mum predictably. 'Have you done your homework?'

Felix mumbles something indistinct but turns the television off resignedly and comes into the kitchen to get his bag. Freddie runs into the lounge and turns the telly back on. I can see him from here. He's thrown himself on the sofa and pulled Felix's duvet over him. Mum sighs.

'Five minutes, that's all, Freddie.'

Honestly, she's so . . . wet when it comes to Freddie. That little squirt runs rings around her. Normally she's a non-stop, inexhaustible bundle of energy, but sometimes

I think Freddie defeats her. It's her own fault for treating him like a baby all the time. She never treated Felix or me like that.

She was pushing it when she had Freddie, she was nearly forty. Luckily I didn't really understand at the time how embarrassing that was.

She sits down heavily at the kitchen table. She looks tired. Come to think of it, she does seem to have lost her sparkle lately. It's probably the menopause. I think that's supposed to make you tired.

'Want a cup of tea, Mum?'

Her head jerks up in surprise. No wonder. Gabby doing caring? Even I don't know where that came from. That little baby on the tube must have brought out my softer side.

'You go and give Felix a hand with his homework in the lounge. I'll bring it in to you,' I say gruffly.

She gives me a small, grateful look and for once in her life says nothing.

It's normal to be embarrassed by your parents. Most people my age complain about their parents, about their dress-sense or the way they dance, or the daft things they come out with in front of your friends or the photos they insist on showing your latest boyfriend of you naked on the carpet as a baby. But all that's par for the course, it's what you expect from parents and actually it's

19

quite endearing and you can have a giggle about it with your mates.

But my parents are not just embarrassing, they're mortifying, in an appalling, blush-making, cringeworthy way. No one believes me till they meet them. Then no one believes I belong to them.

In fact, my whole family is awful. Except for Gran, maybe. She's more on my wavelength. I can cope with her.

I can't cope with my mother and father.

Especially my mother.

Mum is called Posy of all things. Actually that's not her real name, she was christened Pauline, but that doesn't suit her image at all, so she's reinvented herself as Posy. Posy is loud, and large in a windmill sort of way, wider at the bottom with flailing arms that thrash about a lot. She's quite wide at the top too, with a big bosom and a broad pink face that peers short-sightedly at the world through rimless spectacles. I swear she's getting fatter by the day. Maybe she's more like a lighthouse than a windmill because she beams at people all the time and, if that doesn't get their attention, she booms at them like a foghorn, in a rich, plummy tone. Goodness knows where the posh accent came from, Gran speaks with a northern twang. My mother also enfolds people to her bosom a lot which can be quite scary when you meet her for the first time. And, as I mentioned before, she's ancient.

Why couldn't I have had a cool mum like Angie's? She's young and pretty with long dark hair which she straightens and wears back in a pony tail and she's got huge dark eyes with long sweeping eyelashes like Angie's, and great cheekbones. She works in a solicitor's office, even though she left school to have Angie at sixteen. Mum says she's done really well for herself, in her best patronizing voice. When she comes to parents' evenings all the boys fancy her and all the girls drool over her clothes, which are the same as they wear, only they look better on her because she's got a great figure and bags of confidence.

More often than not, Angie's gran comes too and even she looks OK, just normal, middle-aged-smart, and not too conspicuous. Last time, because we were choosing our options for GCSEs, her stepdad came as well and he's cool as, with a shaved head and a black leather jacket and jeans. They all spent ages deciding the best subjects Angie should take. She wants to do something with child-care. What a surprise.

I haven't a clue what I want to do.

Mum and Dad came to the parents' evening of course. It was the highlight of their social calendar, they wouldn't have missed it for the world. They brought Felix and

Freddie with them too. Mum turned up wearing some sort of bright pink and orange patterned tent that actually, I happen to know, cost the earth, but looked hideous, and green wellies with frogs on them because it was raining. I could see everybody nudging each other and giggling.

Dad was in his business suit, all buttoned up and creased around the middle where he's got a load of middle-aged spread. Or, if I'm to be brutally honest, maybe I should say, old-age spread. You see, he's even older than Mum. He's called Leonard and he's a city analyst (don't ask, it's too boring for words) and back in the dark ages he used to be Mum's boss, that's how they met. He looks donkeys' years older than any of my friends' dads. He's going bald – not trendy, shaven-headed bald, but receding, greasy-strands-combed-over-the-skull bald – and he's got a droopy grey moustache and a face like a melted candle, all saggy and lined. When he walks, his head bows gently to one side as if it's too heavy for him and his shoulders droop with the weight of it all.

OK, maybe I am being a bit harsh. I've made him sound horrible. He's not that bad really. It's just that, at the moment, I'm a bit fed up with him. He's not being very much fun.

Felix had his long brown hair tied back in a ponytail that night. Not too bad, but he'd used a scrunchie which attracted a bit of unwelcome attention from the boys, though he sat there in a world of his own as usual and didn't notice. At least he sat still. Freddie was being a pain, running around and crashing into people and generally getting in the way. When we were talking to my form teacher, he was crawling around under her desk and inspecting the contents of her bag as if he was about one year old. Mum was oblivious to it all, rabbiting away loudly to Miss Bell who was obviously more worried about what Freddie was doing rooting round in her personal possessions than my future. Justifiably as it turned out, when he started emptying out her box of tampons on the floor and playing spitfires with them, to everyone's amusement except mine and my teacher's.

'He doesn't understand,' said Mum as Miss Bell snatched them off him and stuffed them back in her bag, her cheeks on fire. Little horror, he understood all right. He's for ever messing about with my private things.

It was a waste of time after that. Miss Bell had lost concentration and obviously couldn't give a stuff what subjects I decided to do next year, she just wanted to get rid of the monster under her desk. I think she may have put me down for Life Skills to get her own back. I'll end up with all the losers.

Outside Dad's car pulls up. Felix is sitting at the table with Mum, his head bent over a book, but I can see his face darken. Mum looks up and glances at Freddie but he's switched off the television without even being asked.

'Bed?' she asks quietly and he nods and gets to his feet. 'Come on, soldier,' she says and picks him up. 'Make Daddy a drink, would you, Gabby darling?'

I go back out to the kitchen without a word. Best to do as Mum says.

Dad's been a bit grumpy lately.

We're all walking on eggshells.

'Cup of tea, Dad?' I ask as he comes through the door, looking knackered as usual. He sighs, puts his briefcase down and doesn't bother to answer, just goes over to the drinks cabinet and pours himself a glass of whisky instead.

Right then, suit yourself!

I've made out my dad's an ogre but he's not really. In fact, up until recently, he'd have hardly been worth a mention. He's a quiet sort of bloke on the whole, in a funny way a bit like Felix in that he's in a world of his own most of the time, only his world is all to do with boring stuff like trading and watching the financial markets go up and down. If I'm honest, he doesn't have that much to do with us. It's Mum who does all the running round after us, he just turns up at school for meetings or concerts when he's told to and every so often notices what Felix is wearing and looks alarmed and says, 'The sooner we get that boy into a decent school, the better.'

By a decent school he means a boarding school for boys, like the one he was sent away to when he was seven. Mum won't hear of it. She's afraid it will arrest Felix's emotional development.

'I want all my little fledglings safe and sound in my own little nest at night,' she says, nauseatingly, whenever the subject's broached.

Little fledgings, my foot! I wish they'd send that great big cuckoo, Freddie, off to boarding school instead and do us all a favour.

'Where's your mother?' Dad asks, sitting down on the sofa next to me and loosening his tie. His hand comes out to pat my knee absent-mindedly, then he tilts back his head and pours the whisky down his throat all in one go. He gasps, sighs again, then rests his head back against the sofa, his empty glass cradled in his hands.

'Upstairs, putting Freddie to bed,' I say but his eyes have closed. He's got big bags under them and he looks so old. I don't know how long he's going to carry on being a city analyst for, I'm sure he's past it, but he shows no sign of packing it in.

It's always been like this but just lately he's got worse. He doesn't do anything else but work, unless you count scouring the financial pages of the papers (broadsheet, of course, not the nasty tabloids) and sampling his wines. He's always been a mild-mannered sort of bloke, but nowadays he gets grumpy over nothing, like Freddie being a pain or Felix saying or doing the wrong thing.

'He's just worried because the footsie's dropped,' Mum says, which would be pretty meaningless to anyone else but we know what she means because we've been brought up with the footsie. In fact, we had a rabbit called Footsie but he dropped dead years ago. Even Freddie understands that she's referring to the FTSE index of leading shares and Dad will be down in the dumps till it goes back up. But then by the time he cheers up, the footsie has usually come down again. It's like he and the footsie are on a seesaw together. Or a rollercoaster, more like. Only they're not having that much fun.

I think Mum's wrong: I think it's old age that makes Dad so bad-tempered. I reckon people over forty shouldn't mix with kids. Our teachers at school are the same: all the old ones are grumpy sods.

Even Freddie's learning to button it nowadays when Dad's around. I glance at Felix. He's got his head in a book. At least he's had the sense to take his Alice band off.

The phone rings and I go to answer it. It's Gemma. I'm not too sure about Gemma. She's one of the gang that gave me a hard time when I first started at the Sec.

She and her cronies, Ruby, Jade and Pearl (known collectively as the Gemstones, how sad is that?), teased me about my expensive, sensible school shoes, regulation black. They teased me about my hair with its straight, heavy fringe, the neat knot in my tie and the name-labels Mum had stitched carefully into my uniform, too. They squealed at the length of my skirt and hooted at my expensive leather satchel, which smelt so gorgeous I couldn't stop sniffing at it. Then one morning they went through it and found my new pencil case and my pens and pencils, all with my name engraved on them, and Gemma broke the nib of my brand-new fountain pen pressing too hard on the first page of my lovely new notebook.

The Gemstones looked like pretty, decorative little jewels, but they were actually razor-sharp weapons that Gemma used to wear me down, scratching and stabbing at me whenever she got the chance. They tried it on for weeks, borrowing my stuff and breaking it, or forgetting to give it back, but they didn't succeed. I didn't cry and I didn't tell on them, not because I was being ultra brave, but because the very first day of school I'd been put to sit next to Angie and we'd bonded together like superglue. There was no way I was going to become unstuck from my new very best friend even if it meant I had to learn to put up with Gemma and the rest of her horrible gang.

You see, I was scared my parents would whip me away from the Sec if I complained because it was actually a mistake I was there in the first place. They'd taken on a huge mortgage to buy our house, for the express purpose of getting me into this new super academy they were supposed to be starting up in the area. Dad had done all the research. They were going to pull down the old Sec and put up a huge, purpose-built, state-of-the-art school. Only Dad was wrong. His grand plan backfired because the academy never got built in the end through lack of funding. So that meant I had to go to the grotty old Sec instead.

Dad really wanted me to go private, he still does, only he doesn't go on about it quite as much now, what with this huge mortgage and the footsie falling. Anyway, I didn't want to go private, not when I had Angie to stand up for me.

'Ignore them!' she said and let loose a torrent of abuse at them whenever they laid it on too much. Angie can be pretty fierce if she has to be, I can see her gran in her. 'They'll soon get bored.'

She was right. They did eventually. When they found out that the Posh Girl wasn't going to snap under their torment, they got fed up and turned their attention elsewhere. And gradually, under Angie's guidance, I learnt to blend in. I hitched up my skirt, loosened my tie, grew my fringe out, ditched the monogrammed pencil case (there were no pens and pencils left anyway) and, to my father's horror, swapped my expensive leather satchel for a backpack. But when I told him it was because I felt sorry for this girl (Gemma, of course, she was the one who'd mocked my satchel most loudly, but it turned out she'd coveted it most) because she was so poor, (not true, Gemma's dad's rolling in it), Mum rushed to my defence and said, 'Oh Leonard, that's so sweet. That's a lovely thing to do, darling, but do ask me first next time.'

To be honest I was glad to get rid of the satchel, it had caused me such grief. Gemma's still carting it around two years later, adorned with the names of all her (in her head) conquests. And I'm glad I didn't tell Mum and Dad what it was like at first because looking back, it didn't take me that long to settle in and now I don't really stand out in the crowd at all, except that I'm always the one who's chosen to make speeches and represent the school and stuff like that. Like, it's so obvious they wheel out the kid with the posh accent.

I like school now on the whole, though if Mum and Dad knew half that went on they wouldn't sleep at night. They're such innocents.

'What you doing?'

'Nothing much. Watching telly.'

I'm still a bit unnerved when Gemma rings me up just for a chat, she's such a hard nut. Weirdly, since I've been in Year 9 she seems to like me. I know I don't look nerdy any more, like I did at the start of Year 7. Angie always tells me I look cool now. I should do too, I work at it hard enough. I buy all the mags to keep ahead of the game, then I pass them on to Angie afterwards.

So I think Gemma's phone calls are actually more to do with *her* feeling a bit lost. We were all taught together in our form groups in Years 7 and 8 but now we're in Year 9 we've been set into ability groups. And Ruby, Jade and Pearl are all in the lower sets. Angie is with me for most subjects but Gemma is with me for *all* of them. It doesn't bother me at all, mixing with a whole lot of new people, though obviously I wish Angie was with me all the time. In fact I like it, because generally everyone's more motivated and we get loads more work done.

It really bothers Gemma though, you can tell. She's like a fish out of water.

'Gabs, I'm having a party, Christmas Eve. D'you wanna come?'

My heart misses a beat. The honest answer to this question is 'No'.

'Yeah,' I hear myself saying. 'Where is it?'

'My house. My parents are out for the evening. We'll have the place to ourselves.'

'Cool.' I'm frantically trying to work out how to get out of this. 'Who's going?'

'Everyone. Look, I've got to go. See you in school tomorrow.' The phone goes dead. I place it back on its cradle then pick it back up again and dial Angie's number. Angie's gran, Mimi, answers. She doesn't sound exactly overjoyed to hear me.

'Gabrielle, is that you? Now, what do you want to speak to our Angelina for? You girls've been together all day and she's not been home two minutes. She's having her tea. Can't it wait till morning?'

'It's about homework . . .'

'Homework my ★★★★,' she says. You can't pull the wool over Mimi's eyes.

'Sorry, Mimi. Tell Angie I phoned.'

'Humph!' she says and hangs up on me. Angie says she likes me, though you'd never guess from the way she speaks to me. But I think Angie's right because she does things like wink at me sometimes when she's going on at Angie about something and she always makes me my favourite hot chocolate with squirty cream and marshmallows when I go there after school.

We're not allowed those in our house. Too much sugar and colouring to wind little Freddie up. That's one of the reasons I'm always at Angie's, if I get the chance.

I'll try Angie on her mobile later. Mum comes

downstairs and smiles at me. 'Dinner time!' she says brightly, looking better now she's got rid of devil-child. I glance into the lounge. Felix is still glued to his book. Dad's slumped on the sofa asleep, his head fallen to one side.

'Dad!' I call. 'Dinner's ready.'

He gives an almighty snore and wakes up. I go to the loo and wash my hands. When I get back to the kitchen, Mum is ladling great lumps of gloop on to our plates and Dad is fishing around in the drawer for a bottle opener, a bottle of red in his hand.

He's a bit of a wine connoisseur, my dad. He's a member of a wine club and when we go to France we have to trail around vineyards with him, replenishing his stock. He says it's an investment but he seems to be spending an awful lot of it lately. We've even got our own wine cellar in the basement. I keep trying to persuade him to convert it into a studio apartment for me but he won't.

I watch as he tugs open the bottle and pours a small glass for Mum, even though she says, 'Not for me!' and a large glass for himself. He takes a big gulp and tops it up. When he sits down he bows his head in his hands, elbows on the table, and for a moment I wonder if he's going to say Grace, only we're not that sort of family. But then he looks up and his hands move down his face, elongating it even more in the process, and finally he rests his chin on his fists and stares at us gloomily.

'Busy day?' asks Mum, placing our plates in front of us with a flourish. 'Never mind. Look what I've made for you. Vegetarian chilli. Your favourite.'

Dad catches my eye and winks, then takes another gulp of wine.

'Yummy, yummy,' I say, picking up my fork and poking tentatively at the grey, glutinous mess of beans, lentils and rice. 'Lucky us.'

Dad snorts mid-swallow and the wine goes down the wrong way. He's off in a paroxysm of coughing, like he's choking to death. Mum bangs him helpfully on the back, pink with concern. Behind them I see Felix in the doorway, attracted by the commotion. I take a forkful of food and start chewing grimly. By the time I've managed to swallow the gluey, grainy mess, Felix has sloped off silently to his room.

This is awful! Angie can't go to the party.

'What do you expect?' she says the next day. 'You know what my family's like. Christmas Eve we all go to church then afterwards everyone comes back to ours and Mimi does a big buffet. We've all got to be there. No one can get out of it.'

I'm not even sure who lives in Angie's flat altogether. There's her mum and her stepdad and her little sister and brother who're not even at school yet, I know that for definite. Then there's Mimi, who I think lives in another flat with Kelvin who's her mum's brother and is actually Angie's uncle but is in Year 11 at our school. Anyway, she seems to spend all her time in Angie's looking after her grandchildren while their mum goes to work. And there are loads more aunties and uncles and cousins who live in the flats too and lots more relatives come and go and it's hard to tell exactly who belongs where.

'I don't want to go if you're not going.' I know I sound pathetic.

'You've got to,' says Angie earnestly. 'Si will be there. I need you to keep an eye on him for me.'

Si is the current object of Angie's affections. Actually, he's the current object of everyone's affections. He's the tallest boy in Year 10 with blond-streaked hair that falls over the most amazing blue eyes you have ever seen in your life and perfect white teeth. He's been out with most of the Year 10 girls, some of the Year 11s, and has now turned his attention to the Year 9s. He's started hanging around with us at lunchtime with some of his mates, fooling about. It goes without saying, it's Angie he's after.

The trouble is, Gemma fancies him too. She makes it obvious, giggling and flirting like mad whenever he comes near.

'She'll get off with him, I know she will,' moans Angie. 'You've got to stop them.'

'How?'

'Talk to him. Keep him occupied. Don't let her get her grubby little mitts on him.'

I can see Gemma the other side of the yard watching us. Next minute she's making her way towards us, cronies in tow.

'I'm not going,' I mutter. 'I'm going to say I'm not allowed.'

'Please, Gabby!' Angie pleads.

Gemma stops in front of us and gives us a cool, appraising look.

'All ready for the party?'

'I can't come,' says Angie quickly. 'I'm really sorry. Family stuff. You know how it is.'

'I know how it is in your family,' says Gemma and gives the others a sly look. They giggle as if she's said the funniest thing ever. Angie glares at them and they subside. Ruby and Pearl live in the same block of flats as Angie so they really know how it is. Their families go to the same church too. I went once, it was really fun. There was loads of singing and swaying and clapping and calling out to the Lord. I wouldn't mind going again but Dad won't let me.

Actually, now I come to think of it Ruby and Pearl will be dragged to church by their mums too, then on to Mimi's for a knees-up. They probably haven't worked out yet how to tell Gemma they can't go to her party.

'Shame,' says Gemma insincerely, actually looking very pleased. 'Everyone else is coming.'

You reckon? I glance from Ruby to Pearl and back again, but neither of them will meet my eye. I look at Gemma's sharp little face and think, everyone's scared of you. Me included.

'Gabby's coming, aren't you, Gabs?'

I hesitate, just for a second, but she's on to me.

'You are, aren't you? You said you were last night.'

Gemma's voice is loud and challenging.

'Course she is. She was just saying how much she was looking forward to it, weren't you, Gabby?'

I turn to Angie, outraged. Her voice is bland but her eyes are pleading.

'Some of the Year 10s are coming. Si and those. Pity you can't make it, Angie,' Gemma taunts.

Angie thrusts her hands in her pockets and looks away into the distance, her jaw tightening. The others exchange a smile but Gemma studies me woodenly, eyes cold, arms folded, waiting for an answer.

I sigh. 'Yeah. I'll be there.'

She smiles. A strange expression floods her face. It's not till later when I think about it, that I realize what it is.

It's relief.

She's a weird one. She's glad that Angie's not coming because it removes the opposition. But why was she so scared that I wasn't coming?

The penny drops. I get it.

She's scared that no one will turn up at all.

I really don't want to go to this party. I try my best to get out of it, but there's a conspiracy against me. I tell Mum about it, expecting her to say something like, 'Oh no, darling, you can't possibly go out on Christmas Eve, I need you to be Santa's Little Helper!' like she did last year when I asked if I could go to Angie's.

But this year she says, 'Whose party?' and 'Where is it?' and when I say, 'Park Square,' she says, 'Oh, those lovely old houses, I didn't know you knew anyone who lives there,' and she looks pleased. I haven't got the heart to remind her it's the girl who pilfered my satchel in Year 7.

'Gabrielle's going to a party on Christmas Eve in Park Square,' she tells Dad, as if it's a fait accompli which it was as soon as she heard it was being held at one of the most prestigious addresses in the neighbourhood.

'Very nice,' he mumbles, and that's it. And it's only Felix who looks at me bemused and mouths '*Gemma's* party?' as if I've taken leave of my senses.

By the time Christmas Eve comes I'm more or less resigned to my fate. It doesn't stop me from feeling nervous though.

'It's not fair,' Angie moans on the phone as I'm waiting for Dad to get the car out of the garage. 'I wish I was going.'

'I wish I wasn't.'

'You'll be fine,' says Angie. 'I bet you look fab in my dress.'

I study myself critically in the mirror. I've made an effort, that's for sure. Well, you've got to, haven't you?

Angie's lent me her black mini-dress with tiny white stars all over it. It shimmers when I move and just about covers my bum. My hair's hanging long and loose down my back and I've put streaks of glitter gel through it so it glows in the dark. I've persuaded Mum to let me wear my main Christmas present too, a pair of designer, tight-fitting, high-heeled black leather boots. They were so expensive, but they're worth it. They make my legs look soooo long and I've still got yards of leg in sparkly tights to show off.

'If you've got it, flaunt it!' instructs Angie. 'Go get 'em, girl! Think of me stuck in with all the rellies.'

At this precise moment I'd give all the pressies under the tree to swap Gemma's party for an evening with Angie's family. And she'd give all of hers to swap places with me. Ironic, or what?

'Gabrielle? Daddy's waiting!' Mum calls from downstairs.

'Got to go. Wish me luck!' I whisper, feeling a bit sick. But then I take a final look at myself in the mirror and in spite of my reservations I feel a small stab of excitement.

I don't look fab; I look stunning. All hair and legs.

'You don't need it! Keep an eye on Si for me!'

'I will. Love ya babe.'

I snap my phone shut, throw my coat on and run

downstairs, slamming the front door behind me, too quick for Mum to give me the third degree about my ultra-glam appearance. Dad's eyes open wide in surprise as I slip into the front seat and he gets a quick flash of thigh but I pull my coat tight around me and he says nothing. Within seconds we're winging our way through the brightly-lit streets, busy already with festive party-goers, and to my surprise I discover I'm actually quite looking forward to my night out.

That's till I get there. Dad pulls up in front of a big stone house with pointed metal railings around it. The house is quite dark but through the windows I can vaguely make out the shapes of people. Gemma's at the door with Jade. Her arm is around Jade's neck and she's got an alcopop in her other hand. Luckily, she hides it behind her back when Dad gets out of the car.

'Da-ad! I don't need you to take me in!'

'Just thought I'd say hello to Gemma's parents. Thank them for inviting you.'

'NO! I'll see you later! Go on!'

He looks a bit uncertain. 'What time shall I pick you up, then?'

'Midnight?'

'Good grief! I was thinking more about ten.'

Behind me, I can hear Gemma and Jade giggling. My stomach lurches. To be honest I wouldn't mind going home at ten. Actually, I wouldn't mind going home at this precise moment. But for appearance's sake, I had to protest a bit.

'Eleven o'clock,' I say firmly. 'And wait outside.'

I wait till he drives away, then I take a deep breath and turn to face the others.

'You coming in then, Gabby?' says Gemma. 'I mean you haven't got long till Daddy comes back to fetch you.'

Jade sniggers.

I grab the bottle from Gemma's hand and take a big swig. 'Least I came!' I say and smile sweetly. 'Ruby and Pearl not here yet?'

Gemma scowls but I slip my hand into my bag and take out the spare pair of earrings I bought on my shopping expedition. I knew they'd come in handy for someone. I've wrapped them up in masses of white tissue paper and tied a red, shiny ribbon round them. I thrust them into her hands. 'Present for you.'

Her face brightens. She tears the paper apart and squeals with delight.

'I love them! Look at these, Jade!' She puts them in immediately alongside the ones she's already wearing, one of the advantages of having lots of piercings, then throws her arms around me. Her breath smells of alcohol. 'Come on, Gabby, let's party!' She grabs hold of my hand. Jade glowers at me but I take a deep breath, toss my hair back and allow myself to be pulled into the house.

Inside it's dark and I can't see a thing for a minute till my eyes adjust. Gemma abandons me straight away. People are dancing. There are not that many there to be honest, five or six girls jigging around in the centre of the room and a few boys standing together munching crisps and swigging from bottles. It's like I thought, most people in my class have found an excuse not to turn up. Flipping Angie! The things I do for you! It's smoky, which I hate, and there's no sign of any grown-ups, but at least nobody's off their head.

'Wanna drink?'

Someone offers me a bottle. It's Si. I can still taste the cloying sweetness of the alcopop on my tongue.

'No thanks. I'd rather have a Coke.'

'Go on, let your hair down!' He treats me to a full-on smile and tries to press the bottle into my hand.

I shake my head. 'I said, no thanks.'

His smile fades.

'Here's a Coke.' Behind him a boy bends under a table and plucks a can of Coke from a cardboard box. He presses it open and hands it to me.

'How's that?' he asks. It's Tug, another Year 10 boy who I've seen around with Si.

I take a sip. 'Perfect.'

He smiles at me. 'Good.' He's not good-looking like Si,

but he's got a wide, crooked grin that lights up his face. I smile back.

'Where's Angie tonight?' asks Si.

'She can't come. Family stuff.'

'Shame.'

I make a mental note to put that at the top of the list when I report back to Angie. She's going to want to know every single detail.

'You look fantastic, Gabby.'

'Thanks,' I say in surprise. I don't think Si's ever really noticed me before, he's only had eyes for Angie. He is gorgeous; I can see what the attraction is. I flick my hair back behind my shoulders and glance around the room.

The next minute Gemma bangs into me. 'Sorry!' she giggles. 'Want to dance, Si?'

'Later,' he says, not even bothering to take his eyes off me. I feel awkward.

Gemma gives us a hard look then she turns to Tug and grabs him by the arm.

'You then,' she says, brooking no argument, and drags him off to the dance floor. As we watch, she drapes her arms around his shoulders and nuzzles her face into his neck. He places his hands awkwardly on her hips, almost as if he's trying to fend her off, and starts to sway in time to the music.

'He looks terrified!' Si bursts out laughing and I can't

help but join in. Suddenly, he puts his arm around my waist and draws me close to him.

'You look older than you do at school,' he whispers.

I giggle nervously. 'Yeah, well, school uniform doesn't do much for anyone.'

'Oh, I don't know . . .' he breathes, 'I wouldn't say that.'

His teeth are white in the darkness of the room. I take an involuntary step back and almost lose my footing. Si catches my hand and steadies me.

'Careful!'

'Thanks,' I say, but he doesn't let go of my hand.

'Want to dance?' he asks.

'All right.' I put down my drink and he leads me into the circle of people dancing and puts his arms around me. I place my hands on his shoulders and move gently in time to the music, horribly conscious of Gemma and Tug next to us. When the music ends I pull back.

'Not so fast,' he says, smiling down at me. 'Stay for another one?'

I look over his shoulder and see Gemma watching us. His arms tighten around me and he joins them together in the small of my back, pressing me closer to him, and the music starts up again. It's a slow one, my favourite. We begin to move together, in rhythm. He's a good dancer. He reaches one hand up to touch my hair, the other presses lightly on the base of my spine. 'Sooo silky,' he croons. I can feel his breath against my neck and his hand stroking my hair and I start to relax and settle into him, at the same time every nerve in my body aware of his touch.

Is this what it feels like to be hypnotized?

I'll never know because the next minute I'm practically knocked off my feet. 'My turn!' announces Gemma, barging her way between Si and me. 'It's my party!'

Her voice is slurred. She turns her back on me and flings her arms around Si's neck and starts a stumbling, slow shuffle. He looks annoyed but puts his arms round her. I retreat back to my drink and Tug follows me, looking relieved. One or two others from my class have turned up and we all get into conversation and the next time I glance at the dance floor Si and Gemma are nowhere to be seen.

And I know I should go and find out where they are because I promised Angie I wouldn't let them get together, but I don't.

Because, the thing is, Gemma's such a slapper, everyone knows that. Si won't stay with her, whatever they get up to.

Perhaps they should just go ahead and get it over and done with.

I think it's better that Si's with Gemma tonight rather than with someone else.

Someone like me, for instance.

Christmas Day in the Sheraton-Hogg household. I forgot to say we have a double-barrelled surname. Well, we would, wouldn't we? Hogg is actually my dad's name, Sheraton is my mum's, not the other way round as you'd imagine. I always thought they were partners in an accountancy firm and when they got married they just put the names together. That's what Mum led me to believe. Only it turns out it wasn't quite like that. Pauline Sheraton wasn't actually an accountant at all, she was merely a humble secretary when she got a job at Leonard Hogg's office and made herself indispensable to the boss.

Poor Dad, I bet he didn't know what had hit him when she arrived on the scene, like a two-ton truck bearing down on him. He didn't stand a chance. He must have been getting on a bit by then and I suspect had led a pretty sheltered life up till that point. Public school, Oxford, the City. Could be exciting, but not in Dad's case.

All that was to change with the arrival of powerful Pauline, a force to be reckoned with.

You know, in some ways, I think my mother and Gemma have got a lot in common. I don't mean Mum's a slapper (well, she might have been, who knows? Yuck, don't go down that path) but they're both mega-good at getting what they want and bulldozing to the ground anyone or anything that stands in their way. (In Mum's case in the nicest possible way of course, though I can't say the same for Gemma.)

Anyway, before he had time to blink (which he does, quite a lot), she'd bundled him up the aisle and got herself pregnant with me. In the process she moved several rungs up the social ladder and acquired a big house and a double-barrelled surname. (Well, she wasn't going to abandon a nice name like Sheraton, for an awful one like Hogg, was she?) That's when she reinvented herself as Posy, which she claims was Dad's pet name for her as she was as pretty as a bunch of flowers. (I don't think so! I've seen photos of Mum in those days and pretty is not the adjective I would ever use to describe her.)

She's never looked back. (I bet Dad has, with longing.) In fact, I think Mum has completely forgotten about her not exactly humble, but certainly not as well-off-as-she-is-now origins, hence the strangely posh accent and the memory lapses in her personal history.

It's always a source of amusement when Grandma comes to visit, especially at Christmas. She brings Mum back down to earth, my gran. Won't let her Pauline get away with what she calls 'her nonsense'.

Dad goes off to fetch her first thing, before the boys are up. Mum likes her to be here for when we open our presents. I think it's a showing-off thing because we always get something outrageously expensive, even if it's not normally what we'd choose ourselves, and Gran tuts in disapproval. It's all part of our Christmas.

'Blooming taxi-service.' I can hear Dad grumbling as I come downstairs, clutching my stocking. 'She's going to have to stay the night. If she thinks I'm going without a drink Christmas Day just to give her a lift home, she's got another thing coming.'

Huh! Fat chance! He doesn't go without a drink any day of the year. He'd even had one last night: when he came to pick me up from the party, I could smell it on him. Has he always been like this?

Probably. But I think he's getting worse.

'Get a move on,' clucks Mum, pushing him out of the door. 'The boys will be up soon. They'll want to open their presents.'

Mum follows me into the lounge to watch me open my stocking. She loves all this. We're too old for stockings really, especially me. In theory, Freddie still believes in Santa Claus, though in practice I know this is highly unlikely because he doesn't believe in anything unless it's completely logical and we don't have a chimney, so he can't.

But I see Santa's been anyway because there are a lot of exciting-looking parcels under the tree and one massive big one that's standing beside it, taking up half the lounge. Impressive, even by Mum's standards. I look at the label. It says, 'For Gabrielle, Felix and Freddie, with love xxx,' in Mum's writing. I wonder what it is. A home cinema perhaps? A trampoline? A snooker table? Some gym equipment? Or maybe a quad bike? That would be really cool! But then we'd spend the whole time arguing about whose go it was.

'Happy Christmas, darling!' Mum envelops me in a big warm hug then perches eagerly on the arm of the sofa while I unwrap the contents of my stocking. Each item is perfectly wrapped in red tissue paper and adorned with gold ribbon and bows. I don't know how Mum finds time to do it. It's the usual stuff: hairslides, a wallet, chocolate, some lippy, a pencil case, earrings, knickers, all very pretty and all that bit too young for me. There's even a pink glitter Tamagotchi, the pièce de résistance I gather, as I see the delighted expression on Mum's face when I open it. Honestly, what's wrong with her? I had one of these when I was about six! You have to spend all your time looking after this weird little character on the screen as if it's your own baby. Like I'd bother! They're expensive too. Next time, Mum, just give me the money, please!

But she's looking at me all bright-eyed and bushy-tailed as if she's made me the happiest girl alive by going out and finding this . . . stuff, so I play along with it as usual and fling my arms around her and say, 'Thank you, thank you, thank you,' so perpetuating the myth that I'm thrilled to bits and ensuring I have to go through the same pantomime next year. She's so well-meaning, I can't bear it.

I glance at the big pressie. 'Looks interesting, Mum. Can I open it?'

'No! It's not just for you, it's for all of you.'

'Can I just take a peek?'

'No!' She's bursting with excitement, she's practically sparking. 'Wait for the boys. Wait for Daddy and Gran. It's a surprise for you all.'

'Does Dad know what it is?'

She shakes her head vehemently. 'Absolutely not. I wrapped it up last night after he'd gone to bed. I had to put it together myself. It took me ages!'

'Is it for him as well then?' That rules out the

trampoline. Maybe it *is* a huge widescreen telly with plasma screen? No, you wouldn't have to put that together. It must be a snooker table. 'You should put his name on it too.'

She frowns. 'Do you think so? Maybe I should.'

'What about Gran? You can't leave her out.'

She hesitates. 'Shall I? Oh dear, I don't know what to do now.'

She's getting all flustered. I laugh. 'Leave it. Gran won't be bothered. Neither will Dad, come to that. It's Freddie who's going to be excited.'

'Yes he is, isn't he? And Felix. And you. You are going to be so thrilled, I know you are! Oh, I can't wait to see your faces!'

My mobile rings. It's Angie, wishing me a happy Christmas. Last night when I got in I rang and told her all about the party, at least up to the moment when Si disappeared with Gemma. I thought it was wise to leave that bit out. I mean, I didn't want to ruin her Christmas, did I?

'What did you get?'

'I haven't opened anything yet. We're waiting till my gran arrives. What about you?'

'A new mobile from my mum, money from Mimi to buy clothes, smellies and stuff from everyone else. It's brilliant!'

Angie never seems to get that much for Christmas and birthdays, not compared to us, but she's always chuffed to bits with what she gets. Instead, her family seems to go more for the food and partying than we do. They have a ball at their place. Our Christmas dining is normally a bit of a non-event: combine Mum's cooking with the fact that Freddie's usually feeling sick after stuffing the contents of his selection box down his throat during the morning and you get the picture.

Actually last year he really was sick. At the dinner table.

'Here they are!' Mum leaps up as Dad's car pulls into the drive. 'Let Christmas begin! Let's get those boys up.'

I open the front door as Mum runs upstairs. Gran's getting out of the passenger seat, her arms full of parcels. She's ramrod thin with neat, iron-grey hair and formal, well-cut clothes. Everything about her is well-proportioned and tidy and she's the most down-to-earth and methodical person I know. You can always find anything you want in Gran's house, whereas in ours nothing is ever in the right place. We get on well, Gran and I, we share an exasperated intolerance of my mother and the same sarcastic sense of humour.

'Happy Christmas, Gran!' She presents her cheek to me and I plant a light kiss on it. No Mum-like all-enveloping embrace from her. She smells of powder and mint mouthwash and her cheeks are dry and withered like apples that have been left in the fruit-bowl too long. 'Shall I take those for you?'

'Might as well. Add them to the rest of the pile. I expect you're looking like Hamley's bargain basement in there.'

'Something like that! There are some very interesting-looking parcels, that's for sure.'

'Never one to do things by halves, your mother,' sniffs Gran. She hands me a silver-foil-covered oven tray. 'Stick these in the Aga. Freddie been sick yet?'

'Not yet.'

'Hmm. Pity. Must be saving it for the dinner table again. It's not nut roast, is it?'

''Fraid so. Mum sent Dad out to buy an organic free-range turkey but he came back without one. Said they were too expensive.'

She sighs. 'Well, at least someone's got a bit of sense. Shame though. Now we're stuck with the veggie excuse for a good feed and all the bits will get under my teeth.'

'Never mind, there's Christmas pudding and brandy butter.' She brightens up. 'Home-made,' I add. Her face falls.

By the time Mum comes downstairs with Freddie in her arms (face by the way already smothered in chocolate, he's obviously been munching his way through the contents of his stocking) and with a sleepy

Felix in tow, I've opened Gran's present to me. It's a CD, this year's chart hits. Hmm. 'Thanks, Gran,' I say and give her a hug. She doesn't respond, she never does, except to say, 'There you are then, I thought you'd like that,' as if that's it, all done and dusted for another year, thank goodness. 'It's for you to play on your new iPod,' she adds, as if she needs to explain her choice.

Felix catches my eye and grins in delight but he's got the sense to say nothing. Freddie hasn't. He frowns and says, 'You don't play proper CDs on an iPod,' then he sits bolt upright in Mum's arms and says, 'What new iPod? Has Gabby got a new iPod? That's not fair, I wanted an iPod for Christmas,' and bursts into tears. Mum cuddles him to her and makes clucky, soothing noises into his neck.

'There, there, Freddie. Maybe Santa *has* brought you an iPod. You haven't looked yet. See the lovely presents he's left for you under the tree?'

Freddie twists around and spots the mound of brightly-wrapped parcels. His wails stop instantly and he pushes himself out of her arms so fast Mum stumbles. He makes straight for the big one by the side of the tree but before he can get his hands on it, Mum yells, 'NO! Not that one. That's not from Father Christmas. It's a special one from me to all of you. We'll open that after dinner.'

Freddie pauses and Mum presses home her advantage.

'Look for one under the tree, Freddie. What about this one?' She lowers herself to the floor awkwardly. 'Do you think this one is iPod-shaped? Do you think Santa's brought Freddie an iPod because he's been such a good boy?'

He had of course, even though Freddie hadn't been the least bit good. He'd brought him an iPod that held up to 4000 songs and 25,000 photos, not that Freddie is remotely interested in either. He's just got to have what Felix and I have. Once he'd opened it, it was thrown aside while he tore open the rest of his presents. He'd opened the lot before Felix and I had even found our iPods.

Poor Felix. He didn't want one in the first place. It's his own fault really. He should have got round to saying what *he* wanted.

Actually, I haven't got a clue what Felix would really want.

Neither has Father Christmas, obviously. Felix is now the proud owner of a rugby ball with G-Spin technology, a pair of leather rugby boots, a holdall with separate hardbase compartment for carrying said rugby boots, a pair of boxing gloves, a good quality willow cricket bat, a set of four stumps and a bail, a proper professional leather cricket ball, a pair of batting pads and gloves and a helmet. He puts the helmet on with its metal three-bar grill and sits there surrounded by the contents of a large sports department, looking like a bemused Hannibal Lecter.

'Everything you need for when you start your new school next year,' says Dad approvingly. 'We'll get you up to scratch by then.'

Comprehension dawns in Felix's eyes. He carries on opening presents – a skateboard, boy-gadgety-stuff, books, games, chocolates – but he looks as if he's shrunk into himself. The only thing he looks remotely pleased about is a beautiful wooden case that opens up to display sets of watercolours, oils and acrylic paints with a range of brushes. Beneath these are two drawers that pull out to reveal colouring and sketching pencils in one and canvas boards and a sketch pad in the other.

'That is gorgeous,' I breathe. He nods, his eyes gleaming at last, and runs his fingers over the smooth wood.

'Let me see!' orders Freddie, with no more presents to open. Felix snaps the box shut and hides it swiftly under a pile of paper. 'That's not fair!' whines Freddie, his eyes falling on the bat. '*I* like playing cricket!'

Gran tuts but nevertheless hands Freddie her present. 'Here you are, Freddie. Maybe this'll make up for your disappointment.'

He tears it open. It's a football annual. It's got a buy-one-get-one-free sticker on it. She hands an identically-wrapped package to Felix.

'Thanks, Gran,' he says quietly and unwraps a rugby annual. Freddie turns a few pages of his book, mildly interested in the pictures, then discards it and looks around for more.

'Say thank you to Gran,' I say crossly.

'Thank you,' he says without even looking at her. 'I'm hungry.'

'Dinner will be soon,' says Mum, clambering to her knees. 'Now don't go filling yourself up with chocolate.'

Huh! Look who's talking! She really needs to go on a diet. Honestly, I don't know if it's what she's wearing today, but she's got a pot on her to rival Dad's beer belly. Gran must think so too because her eyes widen when she looks at her struggling to get up off the floor.

Freddie ignores Mum and opens his selection box and starts stuffing himself. I turn back to my pressies. I've sorted them all out but I still haven't opened them all.

I've got loads as usual. The iPod of course, which I asked for, is not quite as special now my kid brothers have got one each as well, but I do get a new tennis racket which is ace. I get lots of beauty stuff as well, including a facial sauna, a salon-type pedicure and manicure set with rechargeable batteries (Angie's going to love that!), a box of make-up (wrong colours) and a new epilator (useful, though I'd prefer to wax). Gran tuts again when she sees all this and mutters something like, 'Honestly, Pauline, you'll be turning her head!' which is quite an interesting concept if you think about it.

'She's my big girl now,' says Mum and looks on fondly as I open more parcels that belie her words: a cheerleader set complete with pompoms, a shiny diary with a lock and key and a disco karaoke with stand-up microphone, rotating, flashing disco ball and dance-mat. Pu-lease, Mum, how old do you think I am? Felix looks far more interested in all these than I am, not surprising as he *is* ten years old. At last I've finished and I sit there, examining my tennis racket, swamped by my huge pile of pink, glittery rubbish and the contents of Boots beauty counter. Mum watches me with her usual I-hope-you-like-it-I-only-want-to-please puppy-dog expression on her face.

'All right?' she asks anxiously.

'Perfect,' I reply.

'Oh good.' She envelops me in a bear-like Mum-hug. Behind me Gran gives a huge sigh.

And if only Christmas Day had ended at that point, everything would have been all right.

Christmas dinner was predictably awful. Freddie was hyper and wouldn't even sit down at the table till Gran suddenly barked, 'Do as your mother says!' He was so surprised he did as he was told for once. Felix was unusually quiet, even for him, and so was Gran, after her outburst, as if she had something on her mind as well.

Dad didn't even notice, he was too busy opening a bottle of red and a bottle of white for the table and making sure everyone had a glass, except for Freddie, who was actually the only one besides Dad who really wanted one. Mum said, 'Not for me, darling,' but he said, 'I insist!' When Gran placed her fingers over her glass he practically prised them off in order to fill it for her.

I get a 'Good girl,' when I obligingly push my glass forward as he waves the bottle in front of it. He pours a glass of red for Felix too with a 'That'll put hairs on your chest, young man!' I offer up a silent prayer that white wine doesn't have the same effect. Then Dad tops up his own glass again and raises it to the assembled company.

'Happy Christmas!' he says.

'Happy Christmas!' We all echo him obediently and raise our glasses, except for Freddie who's sulking because he's got Coke and Mum who's busy lugging in various dishes from the kitchen.

'Let me give you a hand with that, Pauline,' says Gran.

'No, you sit down. All under control!' trills Mum but it doesn't look under control. Mum has never really mastered the Aga. The roast chestnuts are piping hot and there's steam coming off the mixed swede and carrots in clouds, but the potatoes are looking cold and grey and the rest of the veg, the boiled sprouts and roast parsnips, well, they look sort of wilting and limp, as if they've been hanging around for a long time, unnoticed. The nut roast is dry and burnt at the edges as if it was left forgotten in the oven, which I suspect it was during the mammoth present-opening fest.

Mum flops down at the table and beams at us all.

'Yummy, yummy,' says Dad manfully. 'What a feast! Where's the gravy, mother?' I hate it when he calls

Mum this. She's not his mother, for goodness sake. He thinks it's amusing.

'Oh no!' Mum claps her hand to her mouth, her eyes wide with horror. 'I forgot to make it. I'll make some now.' She jumps up.

'No you won't!' says Gran, grabbing her arm and thrusting her back into her chair. 'You sit down. We can manage perfectly well without it. Have you got any cranberry sauce?'

'I didn't get any,' says Mum, looking mortified, 'what with us not having turkey this year.'

'There's some in the cupboard,' I say, 'left over from last year.' I get up and forage around. 'Here it is.'

'Ugh!' says Freddie. 'I'm not having any. It's manky.'

'Oh dear,' says Mum, looking the picture of misery. 'What shall we do?'

'Mum! No one's died!' I say grimly. The cranberry sauce does look a bit off-colour but I mix it around with my knife and place a little at the edge of my plate. Then someone pulls a cracker and Gran remembers there are pigs' blankets (sausages wrapped in bacon) that she brought over in the oven and everyone cheers up. Soon there are dishes being passed back and forth across the table and everyone has a bit of everything on their plate except for Freddie who decides obtusely that he will just eat pigs' blankets dipped in cranberry sauce, having had a taste and discovered that he likes it after all.

I look around the table. Dad and Gran, wearing paper crowns from the crackers, are devouring their dinner with purposeful, I-was-brought-up-not-to-waste-my-food concentration. As I watch, Dad drains his glass of wine and pours himself another. Freddie and I have refused to put our hats on and Felix has turned one down in favour of a piece of silver tinsel he has tied around his head. He's chasing a potato round his plate with a marked lack of enthusiasm. Freddie has the bottle of cranberry sauce which he keeps dunking sausages into on one side of his plate and a collection of cracker toys on the other, having commandeered them all for himself, except for a miniature sewing kit that Felix has taken a fancy to.

Mum catches my eye and smiles as if we share a secret. Her hat is askew and her cheeks are flushed but her glass of wine is still full and she's hardly touched her dinner.

'Well then,' she says, when the table finally looks like the proverbial bombsite and even Dad can't squeeze any more wine out of the bottle. 'Christmas pud or time for the special present?'

'Special present!' yells Freddie and jumps down from the table before Gran has time to protest.

'Wait!' shouts Mum as he goes to tear the paper off the

massive gift-wrapped parcel beside the tree. 'This one is for all of you. I want you all sitting down properly before we open it.'

Freddie stops, stunned that Mum has actually told him to wait for once. Gran raises her eyebrows at me. I sit down and pull Freddie on to my knees, patting the sofa next to me. 'Come on then, Mum. You sit down too.'

She subsides gratefully on to the sofa. I feel a sudden wave of affection towards her. She tries so hard for us all, she treats the whole business of Christmas like a strategic battle plan where no mistakes must be made, making To-Do lists and shopping lists months in advance. And what thanks does she get? Nothing from Freddie and precious little from the rest of us, if the truth is known.

'What's all this about, Pauline?' asks Gran in a what-have-you-done-now? sort of voice, sitting down the other side of Mum. I glance at her. Be nice, Gran, this is exciting. I can't help still hoping it's a plasma screen TV. My common sense tells me it's not a trampoline or a quad bike which are my favourites, because they're more Dad's sort of presents and when I look at him it's obvious he's not in on the surprise either, he looks as bemused as everyone else. In fact, he looks as if he's thinking, how much is this going to cost me?

'Right then,' says Mum, her voice trembling with excitement. 'This is an extra-special, super-duper, one-off, wonderful present from me to all of you. Well, it's from me and your father actually.'

'Do you know what it is, Dad?'

'Haven't a clue,' he says, bewildered. 'Your mother's lost me this time.'

'Can I open it?' asks Freddie.

'I want all of you to open it,' says Mum. 'On the count of three. Take a corner each.'

This is fun! We jump up and run to the biggest present in the world, tantalizingly covered in pictures of a jolly Father Christmas, and grab a corner each, even Dad. Only Gran stays seated, staring with growing consternation at the festively-decorated object.

'Ready?' asks Mum.

'Yes!' we yell.

'Sure?'

'YES!!' we shout even louder.

'Positive?'

'YEEEEEESSSSSSSS!!!!!!!!' we bawl as loud as we can, so loud my throat hurts.

'Right then. OONE . . . TWOOO . . . THREEEE!!!!'

We tear the paper off shrieking with excitement.

Then we fall silent, a silence which is much much louder than all the noise we've been making, a silence full of astonishment and incredulity, that leaves us goggle-eyed and open-mouthed, a silence that gradually fills with dawning, dumb-striking, thunder-bolting comprehension.

Then Freddie is sick all over the carpet.

I want to die. I want to crawl into my bed and never wake up. I want to throw myself off the nearest cliff and lose consciousness before I hit the bottom. Only there aren't that many cliffs around London.

No, I don't want to die, why should I? None of this is my fault. I want to run away to the end of the world instead and never see my awful family again. My awful mother. Only there's not an end to the world is there? I'd keep on running and find out I've arrived back where I started.

There's no escape.

My mother is pregnant.

She wrapped up our old cot as a Christmas surprise.

I hate her. I hate her pink, grinning, stupid face. I hate her big, round, short-sighted eyes that peer at us anxiously now she's dropped her bombshell and realized, belatedly, that she's blown her whole family to pieces.

How can she be so totally brain-dead that she'd think for one minute we'd be pleased to hear her news?

She's planned this, I know she has, though she makes out it's 'a lovely, lovely surprise!' It's a surprise all right. It's a bloody great shock for all of us, including Dad by the look of him, measuring 8.6 on the Richter Scale.

The trouble with earthquakes of such magnitude is that they don't necessarily have the most obvious immediate surface effect. Apart from Freddie puking up, which to be fair is the result of pigging himself out on toxic cranberries, everyone else just looks stunned. Then Gran suddenly springs into action and grabs hold of Freddie, who's bawling his head off because 1) he's been sick and 2) he doesn't like the surprise present, and hauls him off to clean him up. No one says a thing.

I've read about earthquakes, about the aftershocks. The reverberations come later.

And I'm not just talking subtle tremors here, I'm talking a veritable tsunami that sweeps our family with it in huge, seismic waves.

And I'm not exaggerating.

'I don't know what you're going on about. I think it's lovely.'

'Lovely? How can it be lovely?'

'A new little baby: all soft and cuddly and squidgy; smiley face; tiny little fingers and toes . . .'

'. . . pooey, stinky nappies, smelling of sick; screaming and crying all night long . . .'

'Don't be silly . . .'

'I'm not! I'm remembering what Freddie was like.' I scowl at Angie, who's doing her best to cheer me up. 'I just can't believe my mother's forgotten.'

'They're not all the same,' says Mimi who's cooking ackee and saltfish with fried dumplings at the kitchen stove with Bolton, Angie's half-brother, clinging on to her legs. It smells delicious. Talitha, his sister, is sitting on Angie's knee at the table, cutting pictures of 'pretty ladies' out of magazines.

'Yes they are,' grins Kelvin. He's juggling with bean bags and wandering all over the kitchen as he tries to keep them all in the air. 'I'm with Gabby on this one. Babies don't do anything except cry and poo and be sick all the time. I'm never going to have any kids.'

'Me neither,' I say with feeling.

'When's it due?' asks Mimi.

I shrug my shoulders. 'Not sure. Springtime I think.'

'Why don't you know the exact date?' Angie looks puzzled. 'When Mum had Bolton she knew what day he was supposed to come.'

'Yeah, but he didn't, did he? He was a fortnight late,' chips in Kelvin.

'Well, that's Bolton for you. You're a bit slow, aren't you, mate?'

Bolton rewards her insult with a big beaming smile, loses his balance and sits down heavily on his well-padded bum. A bean bag lands on his head. Everyone laughs.

I love it here in Angie's kitchen.

I wish I could stay here for ever.

I hate it in my house.

At home no one's talking much to each other. Nobody's speaking to Mum at all. Well, Felix never says a lot anyway so he probably doesn't count and Freddie, of course, is his usual objectionable self. But we haven't seen Gran since Christmas Day. I think she and Mum 'had words' because I could hear raised voices in the kitchen while they were doing the washing up and not long after Gran took herself home in a taxi, deciding she didn't want to stay the night after all. There was no point in relying on Dad for a lift since he'd locked himself in his study with a bottle of whisky.

Dad is definitely mad at Mum. Still. They had a huge row on Boxing Day, locked away together in his study. But we could still hear what was going on, because Dad kept raising his voice, even though Mum kept trying to hush him up.

'I warned you how things were!' he yelled and then, 'But no, you had to have your own way as usual!' Later on, just before he stormed out, he shouted, 'Posy! How many times do I have to say this? This could not possibly have come at a worse time!' And I hate to say it, but I had to agree with Dad on this one.

But two days later, Dad sacked the cleaner and I thought that was a bit mean of him. Now, most mornings he goes out without any breakfast and he doesn't come home till all hours.

She should stand up to him but she won't.

'Poor Daddy, he's so busy at work,' sighed Mum this morning. All she'd said was, 'Don't forget it's Freddie's concert tonight, six o'clock,' as he was leaving and he'd turned around and snarled, 'How the hell do you expect me to get there in time? I'm up to my neck in it, thanks to you!' and then went out and slammed the door behind him.

Felix's shoulders hunched up round his neck till his head almost disappeared from sight. Even Freddie went still, staring rigidly down at his bowl. Mum darted a quick furtive look at us to see if we'd noticed but only I met her eye. She gave me a nervous little smile but I was still cross so I ignored her and just carried on eating my cornflakes.

I'm soooo angry with her. No I'm not, I'm absolutely furious. I'm incandescent with rage. I'm apoplectic.

Well, wouldn't you be? If your forty-six-year-old mother was going to have a baby? I mean, work it out, she'll be nearly sixty by the time that poor baby's my age. She'll be practically an old-age pensioner.

I can't believe I said that. *That poor baby*. I don't feel sorry for it, one little bit, I feel outraged by it. How dare it take up residence in my mother's womb? It's too gross for words.

Oh no! My father *will* be an old-age pensioner.

I can't bear it. It's so embarrassing. What could my mother be thinking of?

She made out it was an accident, as if that made it all right. 'I thought it was the menopause,' she says. 'I

73

thought when my periods stopped I was on the change.'

Excuse me! Too much information. You shouldn't even be doing it at your age. It's obscene.

Now I know the real reason why my mother is looking more and more like a stranded walrus; I also know she's going to get bigger and bigger until, eventually, she'll look like a beached whale and then she's going to burst open and bring forth another horror like Freddie to make my life completely unbearable.

I want to leave home.

'Angie?' I say. 'Are you going to leave school after your GCSEs?'

'Dunno,' she says. She's busy helping Talitha negotiate a tricky bit of snipping. 'I haven't really thought about it.'

'I am. I'm going to leave school as soon as I can and get a job. Then I can get my own flat.'

'Your own flat?' Angie looks up, her eyes wide with excitement.

'Yeah. We could get one together if you want.'

'Wicked!'

'You want to stay on, do your A-levels,' says Mimi, wiping her hands on a cloth.

'No I don't. I want to earn money. Be independent.'

Kelvin whistles. 'Go girl!'

Mimi fixes him with her gimlet glare, then turns back

to me, her hands on her hips. 'And what sort of job d'you think you're going to get with no qualifications?'

'I will have qualifications. I'll have my GCSEs.'

Mimi snorts. 'You need a university degree to get anywhere these days.'

'I'll be all right.'

I can feel everyone staring at me. You argue with Mimi at your peril. After a while she says, 'You spoken to your mum and dad about this?'

'No. Why would I?'

Silence. I look up, expecting a mouthful. To my surprise, her eyes are soft.

'Clever girl like you,' she says, 'and my Angelina here. You should go to university, both of you. Then you can share a flat. Study hard, that's what you need to do. Get yourselves a career.'

'Don't see the point,' I say mutinously. I think of the university fund Mum and Dad have been building up for years in my name. Her gentleness throws me and I can feel myself welling up.

'Your father works hard,' she says. 'He's done well. Don't you want to be like him? Go off to work every day in a nice suit with one of them laptops? Have a nice house and car?'

I shrug, fighting back the tears. 'Doesn't make him happy, does it?'

Mimi studies me, then suddenly she bends down and scoops Bolton up into her arms.

'Maybe not,' she sighs, 'but it sure as hell makes him rich.'

At least my news stopped Angie going on about Si for a while, but now we're back at school, she's madly in love again. I was right about Gemma, I think she must have been one of Si's famous one-night stands because they're definitely not together. It didn't seem worth mentioning their little escapade at the party to Angie, especially as I'm pretty sure Si's got Angie in mind for his next conquest. He's for ever seeking us out at breaks and lunchtimes much to Gemma's annoyance.

At last, just when I'm starting to wonder if Si's ever going to make a move, he finally asks her out. It's lunchtime and we're outside the science labs. Angie and Si have been larking about, extremely obviously together, and Tug and I are looking on and at the same time hogging the radiator and trying to avoid being chucked out by teachers into the cold. Just as the bell goes for the end of lunch Si suddenly comes out with, 'D'you girls wanna come down town after school, then? Get a Coke or something?'

'Yeah!' Angie's face lights up. 'We do, don't we, Gabby?'

I hesitate. Is this a double date or are Tug and I just

supposed to be chaperones? I steal a quick glance at him. His cheeks are flushed and he's studying his trainers as if he feels as awkward about this as I do.

Then I remember.

'We can't, we've got French Club.'

Angie's face falls.

'Give it a miss,' suggests Si.

'I daren't,' says Angie miserably. 'My gran'll go mad if I do. She's paid up front for the whole term.'

'She's not going to know, is she?'

Angie looks tempted. 'What d'you think, Gabs?' Her eyes are shining and she looks all excited and hopeful. She never skives her after-school clubs. Neither do I.

From the corner of my eye I notice the Gemstones lining up for Science, obviously earwigging our conversation.

I take a deep breath. I owe Angie. I let Gemma get her clutches on Si on Christmas Eve. She'll be back for more if she gets the chance.

'OK then.'

Gemma scowls.

'Result!' Si punches the air. 'See you later, girls!' He moves off, dancing, down the corridor. Angie watches him, laughing, then turns and flings her arms round me.

'I can't believe it! He's asked me out! What about Tug? D'you fancy him?'

'No way! I'm only doing this for you.'

Too late, I notice Tug still sitting on the radiator, taking all this in. He gets off and slopes down the corridor after Si, his face scarlet. I'm gutted, I wouldn't have said that if I'd known he was listening.

Angie is still in raptures.

'Aw, thanks, Gabby. You're the best friend in the whole world. Love ya babe.'

'Love ya,' I say automatically and give her a quick squeeze. To tell the truth, I'm all churned up inside. I mean, Tug's all right, but I don't want to go out with him. And judging by the look on his face, he feels the same about me now.

Let's face it, he'd probably prefer to go out with Angie than me.

And I'd rather go out with Si.

As it happens, all my worries were in vain. I didn't get to double-date with Tug after all. I come out of school at the end of the day, arm-in-arm with Angie who's lippied, fragranced and mascaraed up to the eyes (literally), and see Si, cool as, leaning on the wall, waiting for us, with Tug by the side of him looking as if he'd rather be somewhere else.

And next to them, perched on the wall like some enormous, moon-faced Humpty-Dumpty, is my mother, wearing a multi-coloured marquee and, for some inexplicable reason, because today it is definitely *not* raining, her favourite green frog wellies. Her hair is tied up in a top-knot with a purple scarf. She looks ridiculous. With her is a disgruntled-looking Freddie and Felix, wearing *his* favourite Alice band.

'Gabb-eeee!' she calls. 'Gabby darling!' She waves furiously as if by some random piece of misfortune I've been struck by amnesia this afternoon and have failed to recognize my family. I can feel ripples of amusement radiating around me, like my mother's some weird sort of wireless frequency that sends out signals of oddness to make people laugh at her. Tug looks at her with incomprehension and I can see Si's lip curling. I don't need to turn around to tell that the Gemstones are enjoying the cabaret, I can hear them sniggering. I debate making a run for it but it's too late.

'Gabby!' she booms, over the heads of the interested spectators milling about the school gate. 'Can you take Felix and Freddie home for me? I forgot I've got antenatal clinic and I'm going to see the midwife today.'

I can sense the swell of curiosity this causes and I actually hear Gemma gasp behind me. Mum, needless to say, is oblivious. Angie takes one look at my face and marches up to her.

'How are you, Mrs Sheraton-Hogg?' she asks with her usual impeccable manners.

'Very well, thank you, Angie,' says Mum. 'Except my feet are swelling. I've got to wear my wellies, they're the only shoes that fit.'

'They're very nice,' says Angie politely. I can hear the Gemstones imploding behind me.

'Why are you sitting on the wall?' I ask coldly.

'I needed to take the weight off my feet,' explains Mum. 'Is that girl all right?' she asks, pointing at Gemma. 'She seems to be choking. Help me down, darling.'

Reluctantly I put out my hand and Mum grasps it and struggles to lever herself off the wall. Goodness knows how she got up there in the first place. She stumbles and Tug's hand automatically shoots out and grabs her by the elbow. Between us both, he and I manage to get her steady on her feet.

'That's better,' she says. 'Thank you, young man.' She turns to Angie and says confidingly, at the top of her voice, 'I'm so excited, Angelina. I'm going to ask the midwife today if I can have a home-birth.'

Call me paranoid but I detect people drawing nearer, straining to hear the next captivating disclosure from my mother's lips. 'I'm thinking birthing pool, you know,' she says, lowering her voice by one decibel which simply has the effect of people paying more attention. 'Strip off, get in and get on with it. Let nature take its course. So much nicer.' She stops and beams short-sightedly at the crowd. 'Goodness me,' she remarks, 'what a lot of children.'

'Sorry,' I say to Angie, grabbing Freddie by the hand and giving Felix a nudge. 'Got to go.' Si's face is a picture of disbelief. I shoot a death glare at my mother. Does she do this deliberately? I will *never* live this down.

'See you tomorrow!' calls Angie as I turn away.

'Felix, come on!' I yell in reply. I'm not intending seeing anyone tomorrow. I'm intending to throw myself off the nearest bridge long before then.

Mum drives past us on the way to the clinic, tooting the horn and waving like mad, but only Felix gives a vague wave back. Freddie's sulking because he's got to walk and I'm too busy mentally debating various ways of doing away with myself. How long would it take to starve to death if I locked myself in my bedroom and refused to come out? Too long. Maybe I should just stick my head in Mum's Aga.

Freddie whinges because his legs are tired and no one's paying him any attention but I ignore him and before long he stops. After a while I realize that Felix is lagging behind, lost in his own thoughts. I stop and wait for him, ready to snap. He's slumped inside his coat, eyes cast down, one hand in his pocket, the other trailing his bag behind him, looking as if he's got the weight of the world on his shoulders.

He looks like Dad.

'What's up, Princess?' I ask quietly. His eyes flicker. When we were little we used to play this game called The Wicked Queen, which was me, and my little brothers were my children who I was cruel to and treated as slaves. It was great, I made them do everything for me.

Freddie, who was not that much more than a toddler then, was a prince, and Felix was a princess. He used to love that game, dressed up in an old pink party dress of mine with a pair of Mum's tights jammed on his head and dangling down his back for long hair. We played that game for years till Freddie grew too old to do as he was told and *he* wanted to be the wicked king.

Or was it until that day when Dad caught us and shouted at Felix for dressing like a girl?

'They still giving you a hard time?'

He shrugs and kicks hard at a stone on the pavement but his chin is a giveaway. It wobbles, momentarily.

Freddie pipes up, 'At playtime they wouldn't let him play. They called him a rude word.' He repeats the word, enjoying the opportunity to use it. Felix flinches.

'Shut up, Freddie,' I say automatically. 'Did you tell anyone, Felix?'

He shakes his head.

'Why not? You should tell your teacher. Or the person on duty.'

'There's no point.'

'Yes, Felix, there is! That's bullying, that is. It's not allowed in schools.'

He says nothing. I want to shake him. I want him to stand up for himself. I want to end his sad, silent suffering. I want to go and personally blitz apart every one of those horrible kids who are so mean to my gentle little brother.

I sigh. 'Were you all on your own then, at playtime?'

'No. I went and played with Freddie and his friends instead.'

'Did you?' I stare at Freddie in surprise. 'Did you let Felix play with you?'

'Yeah.' He looks up at me, puzzled. 'Of course I did. We played wild horses. Felix was the bucking bronco. It was ace.'

'That's all right then, isn't it?' I squeeze the hand of my annoying younger brother with a sudden burst of affection and slip my arm around Felix. 'We princes and princesses must stick together.'

'Remember that game we used to play?' says Freddie, his face suddenly alight. 'The Wicked Queen! Can we play it again?'

'I could be the princess!' says Felix.

'And I could be the wicked king!' shouts Freddie.

I look at my two brothers, their faces shining up at me. For the first time I can see a likeness. But Felix is four years older than Freddie. He'll be going to the Sec in September. If he's having a hard time at primary school, he'll have an even worse one there.

'No,' I say regretfully. 'I think we're all a bit old for that game now.'

* * *

Dad's home early tonight. He looks even more grumpy than usual, if that's possible. As soon as he's through the door he goes straight to the drinks cabinet, pours himself a whisky and tosses it back. Then he pours himself another one and slumps in his chair, staring at the television in brooding silence.

'Do you want a cup of tea, Dad?' I ask, feeling uncomfortable, but he just grunts. I get up off the sofa where I've been watching telly with Freddie and go into the kitchen to make one anyway, just to get out of his way. By the time the kettle's boiled, Freddie has sidled in after me.

'I'm hungry,' he whines. 'Where's Mum?'

'Gone to see the midwife, remember?'

He doesn't reply, just picks at a corner of the wallpaper that is coming away, just below the tiles.

'Stop doing that,' I say automatically. He turns his back on me and picks his nose instead.

'I can see what you're doing.'

He turns around and scowls at me. For a second it's like looking at a mini-version of my father, then I notice his bottom lip is trembling and a tear is rolling down his cheek. I put down the spoon and stretch out my hands.

'Come here,' I say. 'Give me a cuddle.'

He flings his arms around my waist and I press him

close, stroking his blond, silky hair. I don't know how much he really understands about Mum having a baby. She's explained it all to him, of course, in her own unique way, a convoluted mixture of storks, gooseberry bushes and far too much gynaecological detail. I reckon the poor kid is totally confused.

'She won't be long,' I say and plant a kiss on his head.

'Will she bring the baby back with her?' he asks in a small voice.

'Not today,' I say and he looks up relieved and rewards me with a watery smile.

'What's wrong with him?' Dad's standing at the door. Freddie tenses, but I keep my arms around him.

'Nothing. He just wants a cuddle.'

'Leave him alone, you're as bad as his mother. You'll make a flipping pansy out of him. Just like his brother,' he adds in an undertone.

Freddie wriggles free. 'It wasn't me,' he says sulkily, 'it was Gabby. She made me.'

I gasp at the unfairness of it all. Dad shakes his head and turns to go but he comes to an abrupt halt. Felix is in the doorway. He's wearing Mum's pashmina and it falls in graceful drapes around his shoulders, making his face soft and mysterious.

'Look at me, Gabby,' he says, twirling around. 'I'm a beautiful eastern princess. Come on, let's play The

86

Wicked Queen.'

'GET THAT THING OFF YOUR HEAD!' bellows Dad.

Felix snatches the shawl off, his eyes round with shock. Dad glares at him then barks, 'Where's your mother?' Freddie shrinks back behind me, gripping my arm tight.

'Gone to antenatal,' I say.

Dad runs his hands through his hair and swears out loud. The boys stand there with their eyes glued on him, riveted to the spot.

'Go to bed!' he yells at them. 'Now!'

Felix scarpers upstairs immediately but Freddie turns to me and whispers urgently, 'We haven't had our tea yet!'

'That's OK, I'll bring some up to you. Go on!'

He nips past Dad without a word as if he's scared Dad's going to yell at him again but he needn't have bothered. Dad's temper subsides as quickly as it flares up, like flood water seeping back into the earth now it's wreaked its damage. He stands there with his hands in his pockets looking as if he doesn't quite know what to do next. He's like the forgotten Christmas balloons above the kitchen door, crumpled, deflated, empty . . . useless.

I turn my back on him, busying myself with the toaster, opening a can. By the time I've loaded up the tray with two plates of beans on toast, he's disappeared.

Upstairs Freddie has put on his pyjamas and is under his duvet which is amazing in itself. Mum usually spends ages coaxing him into bed. But as I push the door open noisily with my foot, I see his little face, peaky with anxiety, and I say, 'Pizza delivery!' and his face lights up and I say, 'Only joking!' but he laughs anyway and falls on the food as if he's starving to death. I leave him stuffing himself and take the other plate into Felix's room. He's sitting on the floor with his new box of colours open in front of him, sketching.

'All right?' I ask.

He nods without looking up.

'I've got you some tea.'

'I'm not hungry.'

'Don't be silly, you've got to eat.' I plonk the plate down next to him but he carries on sketching.

'What are you drawing?'

'Just stuff.'

I take a peek. He's drawn a picture of a wicked king with great big boots stamping on a tiny princess. The king has a droopy moustache.

'That's good.'

It is. The resemblance to Dad is unmistakable. Felix selects a grey crayon and starts colouring in the moustache.

'I'll leave you to it then.'

'Gabby?'

'What?'

He carries on colouring in, in careful, deliberate lines. 'Why did Dad yell at me?'

I sit down on the edge of his bed. 'He's just in a bad mood.'

'But I didn't do anything, Gabby.' His brow furrows. 'Did I?'

I sigh. Poor Felix. 'I don't think Dad likes you dressing up, Fee.'

He falls silent. After a while he says, 'I don't think Dad likes me full stop.'

The front door bangs. 'I'm home!' shouts Mum. 'Where *is* everybody?'

'Coming down?' I ask Felix. He shakes his head and selects a black crayon.

'Well, don't forget to eat your tea then,' I say and he nods, but at the door I look back and he's busy colouring in the Wicked King's boots with heavy, black strokes.

I look in at Freddie. To my surprise, he's already fast asleep, flat on his back, arms up by his head, as if he's being held at gunpoint, bean-juice staining his chin. I tuck in his sheet which is trailing on the floor and pull the duvet over him, feeling a surprising wave of tenderness. He's got his good points, I suppose.

Downstairs, Mum is sitting on the sofa with her feet up. She looks tired.

'Daddy not home yet?' she asks.

'He *was* here,' I say. 'He must be in his study.'

Mum frowns. 'Where are the boys?'

'Bed. They've had their tea.'

'Splendid.' She looks relieved at not having to face the nightly performance with Freddie. 'Did Daddy put them to bed?'

'No, I did.'

'Oh.' She looks disappointed momentarily then says, 'Thank you, darling, that's good of you.' She sighs. 'I've just been told to rest more at the clinic. My blood pressure's too high.'

'What's that mean?'

There's a pause, then she says, 'Nothing much. Sometimes I think they look for things to say. I asked if I could have a home-birth and I don't think they're too keen.'

Thank goodness for that! 'Why not?'

She pulls a face. 'My age, I guess.'

At last! An acknowledgement that Posy Sheraton-Hogg might actually be just a teeny bit too old to be having a baby. But then she goes on, 'I've made up my mind though. I had you three at home, I don't see why this one should be any different.'

No, you wouldn't, would you? 'Did you have Freddie at home? I can't remember.'

'That's because you and Felix went to stay with Gran.'

'Did we?'

'Yes, you didn't want to come home if I remember rightly. Ouch!' She rubs the side of her belly.

'What's the matter?'

'She's kicking. Feel?'

I shake my head, feeling a bit sick. Why would I want to feel something wriggling around in my mother's stomach? Then I take in what she's just said.

'Is it a girl then? Do you know what it is?'

She smiles. 'No. I could have asked but I'd rather wait and find out when it's born, like I did with the rest of you. I don't know, maybe it's wishful thinking, but I always think of this baby as my little Clover.'

'Clover?'

She doesn't hear me. She strokes the mound of her stomach lovingly, absorbed in something I can't see, can't feel.

I'm jealous.

How can I be jealous of a foetus?

'What would you like it to be?' asks Mum.

Non-existent. But I can't say that, can I? I shrug.

'A baby brother or sister?' Mum probes.

'Don't care.'

She looks disappointed then she says, 'That's all right then.'

I do care though. I hope it's not a girl. I don't want a baby sister. I don't want a baby brother, come to that, but I definitely don't want Mum to have another daughter. I'm the special one round here.

The door opens and Dad comes in. He sits down and opens the paper, like a barrier between us. 'What's for supper?' he says grumpily.

Mum sighs. 'I'll go and sort something out.'

'Good,' he says, turning the pages. After a moment he gives a little cough and says, 'In your own time.'

Mum struggles to her feet and disappears into the kitchen. I feel the anger rising up inside me, till it fills my throat, threatening to choke me. I mean, I'm not exactly the most long-suffering of people and I've definitely earned my brownie points today, bringing the kids home when I could be on a date, making them tea, keeping them out of his grumpy way. And what about Mum? School run, dashing off to the clinic, *pregnant*, and him just sitting there, expecting her to wait on him, hand and foot. Just who does he think he is? Suddenly, I just can't help myself, I jump up and grab the stupid paper from his hands, tearing it in the process.

'She's got high blood pressure you know!'

He stares at me in shock. For one awful second I wonder if he'll hit me though my father has never hit me in my life. Then his face falls.

'*She's* got high blood pressure!' he complains. 'Well, join the gang. And that's the least of *my* problems!'

He grabs the newspaper back and shakes it out, re-erecting his defence against the world. I treat him to my best evil face, wasted because he can't see me, and go out to the kitchen to give Mum a hand.

I'm finally going on my first date. It's not just my first date, it's my first double date. Si's asked Angie and me to go out with him and Tug, properly this time, in the evening. I don't want to, not really, not with all the stuff going on at home, but Angie's kept on at me so much I've got to. She's so in love with Si and it's not as if I find Tug repulsive or anything. It's just that I wanted my first date to be really special.

We get ready at my house. Angie's so excited I have to keep reminding her to tone it down. As far as my parents are concerned, we're going to the cinema – just the two of us.

'Do you need a lift?'

'No thanks, Dad, we'll be fine.'

'Do you want me to come and pick you up at the end of the film then?'

'No, I'll get a taxi.'

He looks relieved. Well, he would, wouldn't he? I mean, he wouldn't want anything to interfere with his daily alcohol intake. To be fair, he is making an effort. I think he's ashamed of his outburst the other night. He hands me a tenner and then, prompted by Mum, he offers one to Angie too, but she refuses. Then Freddie asks for one and Dad pretends to box with him and everyone laughs.

You'd swear we were a normal family.

I pocket the tenner, though I intend to walk home anyway. He can afford it.

'Not long now,' says Angie as we go out into the dark night.

'What?'

'Your mum. She looks really tired.'

'Does she?'

'Yeah. Gabby, d'you go round with your eyes shut?'

'I know she's knackered, stupid.'

'She looks ready to drop if you ask me.'

'Yeah well, I didn't. She's got ages to go.'

'All right, grumpy clogs.' She puts her arm through mine. 'Don't fall out with me. *We* are going to have the best night ever!'

She frogmarches me to the cinema but when we get there, there's no sign of the boys. This is hardly surprising since we're about ten hours too early (OK, ten minutes), but Angie takes this to mean they're not coming at all.

'Perhaps we've got the wrong place,' she frets, standing on tiptoe and peering up and down the street, like one of those meerkats, all long neck, jerky movements, rounded, anxious eyes. I lean back against the wall to catch my breath.

'Angie, there *is* only one cinema,' I point out, wheezing gently.

'Perhaps he's changed his mind. Maybe he's gone off me already! Gabby, d'you think he's dumped me?'

'No, not yet. That would be a record, even for Si. He dumps you *after* a date, not before.'

'Where is he then? He's not coming, I know he isn't. What are you *doing*?' This last because I've slumped to the ground and am sitting with my back against the wall.

'I've got a stitch!'

'Get up, Gabby. We've got to go!'

'What?' I say, startled. 'We've only just got here.'

'I know that, idiot, but we can't be seen waiting for them. That would be too sad for words. Come *on*, Gabby, they'll be here in a minute!'

'I thought you said they weren't coming,' I grumble, but I do as I'm told and get up and follow Angie as she disappears back around the corner. 'How far are we going?' I yell as I see her legging it up the road. If she was a bit closer I'd tell her that I'm pretty sure I've just seen

Si and Tug getting off a bus opposite the cinema but she's going so fast she's out of earshot. I stop under a streetlight, pull my phone out of my pocket and text her the information, then sit down on someone's front wall to wait. Within minutes she's back.

'Are you sure?' she says in a hushed voice.

'Yes. What are you whispering for? They can't hear you, they'll be waiting for us outside the cinema.'

She grabs my arm, looking as if she's about to have a seizure. 'Oh my goodness, Gabby, they've turned up! What shall we do?'

'Go and meet them?'

I shake her hand off. To tell the truth, I'm not as cool with all this as I'm making out. I mean, it's all right for Angie, she knows Si wants to go out with her. Whereas Tug . . . well, let's face it, he's just been dragged along like a spare part, kicking and screaming, to make up a foursome, and what for, anyway? Like Angie wouldn't have gone out with Si if he'd asked her on her own. I feel a bit stupid, like I'm not really necessary.

Now she knows they've turned up, Angie loses her nerve completely. She pulls out her make-up, renews her lippy, blusher and eyeliner under the street lamp, scrunches up her curls and spritzes herself fragrant for the umpteenth time, but then she sits back down and wants to wait until she's counted down 600 seconds (ten minutes) after we're supposed to be meeting them, in case we look too keen. We would have been there till morning only, fortunately, the woman whose wall we're sitting on comes out and tells us to get lost because Angie's counting is interfering with *EastEnders* and she's only got to 378, so Angie springs up and says, 'Right, it's now or never,' and tucks her arm through mine and saunters round the corner as if she hasn't got a care in the world.

Si's leaning against the wall and he's smoking (Yuk! Glad I've not got to snog him!) but he flicks the cigarette into the gutter when he sees us and moves forward to give us both a peck on the cheek. How cool is that? (Though I can smell the smoke, not nice.) Tug sort of hangs back and mumbles, 'All right?' which suits me fine, because I've just had a horrible thought that maybe *he's* expecting me to snog *him*, but he looks so much like he's wishing he were somewhere else I realize that's not going to be on his agenda for the night. Fortunately, Si starts banging on about the film which apparently he's seen twice already.

'Who did you come with before?' I ask and he winks and treats me to one of his full-on grins.

'That would be telling,' he says and Angie's face drops but then he says, 'After you, babe,' because at last we're at the front of the queue and she delves into her bag for money. Si goes next then I'm just about to step forward to pay for my ticket when Tug makes a funny noise in his throat and says, 'Let me get this,' and thrusts a tenner at the woman behind the counter. I stare at him in surprise.

'Are you sure?' I ask. His face is bright red and he mumbles something which I don't catch. 'Thanks,' I say and run a practised eye over the stuff for sale. 'Want some popcorn?'

'All right,' he says, which seems to be the only conversation he's capable of this evening. I buy two large cupfuls and hand one to him.

'Where's mine?' asks Si, who's waiting at the door with Angie to go in.

'Buy your own,' I joke, but offer him the cup anyway. He takes some but looks a bit put out.

Inside the film has already started, thanks to Angie making us late, but Si strides confidently down the aisle in the darkness and we all scuttle blindly after him. He can see in the dark like a bat . . . or a rattlesnake. Don't they go hunting at night? Just like Si! Suddenly he comes to a halt and we collide and it gives me an excuse to start giggling till I'm hushed angrily by the audience.

'Spaces over there,' he says and stands back to let me go first but it's Angie who whispers, 'Excuse me,' and squeezes past the line of people who tut and grumble and stand up begrudgingly, grabbing at their coats and bags as they fall to the floor. Si slips in next, then me, then Tug. Soon we're all sitting in a row, following the antics of some guy who can teleport himself through time and space, which is handy because he's trying to escape from some madman hell-bent on murdering him, but he's not very good at it because he keeps turning up in the middle of infernos, floods, earthquakes and raging battles. It's all a bit far-fetched for me, I'm not really a fantasy freak. I think Si's getting a bit bored third time round too because he keeps nicking my popcorn. Normally, I'd object, but 1) I don't want to upset any of the audience any more, especially as they obviously find Teleport Man's actions totally riveting and 2) it's kind of cute the way he helps himself and then looks at me apologetically every time with that cheeky grin of his.

Soon my popcorn's finished. After a while, I realize Si and Angie are having a bit of a cuddle so I keep my eyes firmly glued to the screen, tense with embarrassment. Honestly, I'm not into this double-dating at all. What if they get carried away? What if Tug gets the same idea? I risk a peek at him. He's following the film spellbound and is definitely not about to make a move so I relax. Soon, I'm drawn into the film, despite myself, and I lose all sense of my surroundings.

Which is why, I suppose, it's such a shock when it happens. I mean, it's not exactly hardcore is it, someone holding your hand in the cinema, but I wasn't expecting it, immersed as I am in the celluloid world of good guy versus evil baddies.

I know what you're thinking. Boy asks girl out on a date. Takes her to the cinema. Pays her in. Holds her hand. What's the big deal, Gabby? Even if Tug is not your number one choice of date you can go along with it, can't you? This is the twenty-first century, you know.

Only the thing is, it's not Tug who's holding my hand in the darkness.

It's Si.

I don't know what to do.

I don't know what to say.

I do nothing.

I say nothing.

I just sit there in the darkness, my hand, still as stone, encased in his, staring at the screen. After a while he slides his fingers between mine so they're entwined and starts to stroke my palm with his thumb, slowly, rhythmically, hypnotically. I can't help it: my fingers respond and curl tightly round his.

On the screen, Teleport Man is transporting again, spinning round and round, faster and faster, until he becomes a blur, then a blot, then a single dot and zooms off into the stratosphere.

I am transporting too.

No one knows. Except Si.

What am I doing?

What is he playing at?

I disentangle my fingers and risk a quick look. His arm is around Angie and she's cuddled into him; I can hardly see her. He turns to me and winks. I clamp my hands together and stare blindly at the screen.

When we come out it's tipping down with rain and the wind is icy. None of us are dressed for the weather.

'What shall we do?' asks Tug, turning the collar up on his thin jacket. 'Go for a burger?'

Angie shakes her head. 'I can't. I've got to get home. I mustn't be late.'

Tug turns to me. 'Shall I walk you home?'

I hesitate. 'How are you getting home, Ange?'

She shrugs and looks hopefully at Si but he's retreated into himself against the biting wind, his arms clenched tightly over his chest, his hands up inside his armpits, seeking warmth.

Rain is dripping down my neck and it's wrecking my new shoes. I make a decision. 'Let's get a taxi.'

Tug looks a bit worried as if he hasn't got enough money and I say, 'It's OK, I'll pay.'

'Can't let you do that,' says Tug but Si is already flagging down a cab.

'In that case,' he says cheerfully, 'we'll all come.'

We pile in and have a brief discussion about who's

going to be dropped off first – we all live in different directions. Si takes charge.

'Angie first.' He rattles off the address to the cab-driver.

When the taxi drops Angie off, Si gets out to give her a goodnight kiss. I turn away. The next minute he jumps back in and says, 'Right, mate, you next?' and gives Tug's address to the driver. When we stop, Tug gets out and fishes in his pocket for some change but I say, 'No, don't. You paid me in,' and he says, 'Are you sure?' and I say, 'Of course.' He smiles at me and I think he's nice when he smiles and then I remember I thought that once before at the party.

He stands there for a second on the pavement and suddenly I know that he's wondering whether he should kiss me goodbye and it's one of those awkward moments because I don't know how we're going to do this, whether he's going to lean into the taxi or whether I should get out on the pavement like Si did.

But then Si comes to my rescue because he says, 'See you, mate!' and grabs the handle and slams the door shut. The taxi pulls away. Then, before I realize what's going on, he's sitting next to me and his arm is around me and his lips are on mine and he's kissing me. And then, I can't believe I'm doing this, I'm responding, I'm kissing him back. I can't help myself, anyone would, this is Si, everyone loves Si, Gemma loves Si, Angie loves Si . . .

I come crashing to my senses. What the hell am I doing? Angie is the best friend I've ever had. I draw back in horror, just as the taxi pulls up outside my house.

'What's the matter?'

'Don't tell her.'

'Tell who?'

'Angie! Don't tell her . . . you kissed me.'

'Now why would I want to do that?'

He pulls me back to him but now I resist.

'Promise me!' I say urgently. Angie and I are inseparable. We're going to be flat-mates some day.

'Promise.' He's laughing at me. His head dips towards mine. 'Just one more . . .'

I shake my head blindly and climb out of the cab, closing the door behind me. He opens the window.

'Don't pretend you didn't like it,' he says quietly. I turn away.

'Gabby?' he calls.

'Stick with Angie,' I say, over my shoulder.

'No, listen . . .'

'What?' I turn back to face him.

'I need some money.'

My mind is blank.

'The fare?' he prompts.

Silently I open my bag and hand him the ten-pound note Dad gave me.

'Keep the change,' I say and turn away. Through the open window I hear the taxi-driver chuckle.

'You jammy beggar,' he says. 'You've got it made, son.'

Inside, the house is quiet. No television noise, no sound of someone talking on the telephone, no, 'Is that you, Gabby? Did you have a nice time?' Mum's gone to bed.

In the lounge, Dad is snoring in the armchair, his legs stretched out in front of the gas fire, an empty wine bottle on the table next to him. He's fallen asleep holding a glass, but luckily it's empty because it's lying upended on his chest with just a thin trickle of the dregs staining his shirt. I take it from his unconscious hands and place it on the table, debating whether to wake him or not to tell him I'm home. I decide against it. His mouth is hanging open and his face is etched with deep lines. He looks exhausted.

Upstairs, Mum is a silent mound in the middle of her bed so I don't disturb her either, mindful of Angie's comment that she's looking tired. Freddie is fast asleep too, his bed looking as if he's had a fight with it, the duvet on the floor, a tumble of sheets twisted around his small body. Sleep has washed the crossness from his face and he looks softer and younger somehow. I pull the duvet back over him. What is it about a sleeping child that makes you want to protect them, even one as objectionable as Freddie?

There's a light on under Felix's door. I knock and peep inside. He's on the floor, sketching. He looks up alarmed, closing his sketch pad quickly, but relaxes when he sees it's only me.

'What you doing?'

'Drawing.'

'Can I see?'

He hesitates, then says, 'OK,' and opens the pad. He's drawn a series of women, long-legged and graceful, their hair piled up on top of their heads, with tiny features and long sweeping eyelashes. Each one is wearing something different. One is in a ball-gown, another in a business suit, a third in a flimsy summer dress, a fourth in a tight top and cut-offs, tied daintily at the knee. When I look closely I can see the clothes all have something in common, a pattern of tiny white daisies on each one, that links them all together. It's even picked out on the pockets of the business suit.

'These are really good, Fee!'

'D'you think so?'

'Definitely. I wouldn't mind wearing them myself.'

He looks pleased. 'They're for my new spring collection.'

Something in his voice makes me study him closely. 'Have you done some of these before?'

'Yeah, tons. D'you want to see?'

He scrambles up and goes to his bookcase where he takes out a scrapbook and hands it to me. Inside are pages cut out of the Sunday supplements and Mum's clothing catalogues, showing long, skinny models showing off the latest designer fashions. Alongside them are Felix's own pencil sketches, fluid and assured, showing a version of the same clothing in a more childish but distinctive style. I thumb through the book, pausing to admire a dress here, a top there, all of them sketched on to the same long-legged, long-lashed and instantly recognisable mannequins.

At the back, in large round letters is the title, 'My Winter Collection, by Felix', followed by twenty or so versions of them wearing a whole range of jumpers, tops, trousers, dresses, hats, coats and boots, each of them with some sort of variation of a jigsaw design on them, either in cut or in pattern. They are seriously weird and seriously beautiful.

'These are amazing!' I breathe. 'I didn't know you could do this!'

'I do it all the time,' he says simply. 'It's what I like doing best.'

'You should show these to someone.'

'Who?'

'Dunno.' I pause to think. 'Your teacher? Mum? Dad?'

The light goes out of his face. 'Nah,' he says, taking the book from my hands and putting it back on the shelf. 'It's all right. I'll just keep it to myself.'

You're ten, I think. When did you learn to be so grown up?

My phone bleeps. It's Angie texting me.

Wow! I'm in luuuuve!!!! Do you think he'll ask me out again?????

I sigh deeply and press reply, typing in one single word.

Yes.

'You all right, Gabs?' Felix's eyes are round with concern. Why can't all boys be as nice as my kid brother?

The trouble is, it's not the nice ones you fall for, is it?

I never knew there was so much to having a baby. It's crazy. I thought you just went into hospital, did what you had to, and came out with a sweet little baby wrapped up in a shawl. Nice, clean and tidy.

No way.

That's far too easy for Mum. Not the Posy Sheraton-Hogg way of doing things at all. She's definitely decided to have it at home.

'Why?' asks Gran, who's popped around with some little matinee jackets and hats she's knitted. They're so tiny! Mum says thanks and puts them to one side, hardly bothering to look at them. I know she's bought cute striped babygros and matching little beanies and sleeping bags from the posh new baby shop in town because she showed them to me. I get the feeling Gran's little woolly jackets and bonnets won't see the light of day. Gran looks a bit hurt, as if she thinks the same.

'It's better all round,' says Mum emphatically. 'Less painful, less intrusive . . . I've done it before, remember! I know what I'm talking about.'

'You were a lot younger then. Things can go wrong you know.'

'Like what?' asks Felix, looking worried.

'Nothing will go wrong!' says Mum. Gran gives her a sceptical look. 'And if it did . . . and it's not going to . . .' she continues, 'I'll have two midwives here with me all the time. That's more attention than I'd get in hospital.'

Gran looks worried. 'They're all geared up there, Pauline. It's the safest place.'

Mum's face softens and she leans over to pat Gran's hand.

'I'll be fine, Mum. It's what I want.'

'What you want!' snaps Gran. 'It's all about you, as usual.'

Mum recoils as if she's been slapped.

'I've made up my mind,' she says. 'I'll be more in control. I'll have more privacy . . .'

'Privacy!' barks Gran. 'How can you have privacy in this house! What about the children?'

'That's the point,' says Mum, going pink, which she always does when she's upset. 'They'll be involved, right from the start. All the way through if they want.'

'What do you mean?' I ask, hoping it isn't what I think she means. It is.

'You can be there for the birth if you want. Would you like that?'

'You must be joking!' I can feel my lip curling in horror. My mother has finally flipped her lid.

'See?' Gran looks triumphant.

'I wouldn't mind,' says Felix.

Mum flashes him a grateful look. 'I'm not going to *make* them! It's just that if they want to see their sister or brother being born, I won't send them away. I don't want any secrets in this family!'

'Oh Pauline, for goodness sake!' spits Gran, getting more and more furious by the minute. 'Some things are meant to be kept secret!'

'It's my body and it's my choice.' Mum sounds at total odds with her appearance, like someone my age. Gran has this effect on her.

'And what about Leonard?' snarls my Rottweiler grandmother, refusing to let go. 'Doesn't he have a say in this?'

'He's on your side, Gran,' I put in. 'He's totally against the idea.'

'Of the home-birth? Or the baby?' rejoins Gran, sharp as a knife. All goes quiet. I take a peek at Mum who looks really upset. It's Freddie, who's remained uncharacteristically quiet through the whole argument, who finally breaks the silence.

'The baby, of course,' he states in his imperiously clear voice. 'Nobody wants it, except for Mum.'

When Gran leaves, Mum bangs about in the kitchen for a while then she pokes her head into the lounge where I'm sitting half watching a boring Rambo DVD with the boys (Freddie's choice). 'I'm popping out for a minute,' she says.

Three pairs of eyes gaze at her in surprise. Mum never goes out of the house at the weekend without trying to make it a family occasion.

'Where?' asks Felix.

'Town. Baby shopping,' she adds with a touch of defiance.

Freddie scrambles to his feet. 'I'm coming!'

'No! I won't be long, I'll take the car.'

'I'm hungry!' he whines.

'There are sandwiches and crisps in the kitchen. Help yourself.'

The door closes and we stare at each other, then Freddie makes a bolt for the kitchen to make sure he gets first choice.

After we've finished eating, Dad comes in. Early this morning he'd got up and gone into work, unusually for a Saturday. I thought he'd be gone all day.

'Where's your mother?' he asks.

'Gone baby shopping,' says Freddie, his eyes glued to the battle on the screen. He shouldn't be watching this, it's far too violent. Dad doesn't even notice; he just grunts and sits down, reaching out for the paper.

'There's some lunch in the kitchen,' I say helpfully. I debate offering to get him a sandwich but he ignores me, lost behind the pages of the *Financial Times*, so I think, get it yourself, you ignorant so and so. Why should I run after him like Mum does? After a minute, Felix gets up and sidles out of the door. It's not his sort of film, I know, but I can't help noticing recently that he never lasts long in a room once Dad comes in. I pick up the empty crisp packets and crumb-filled plates and take them out to the kitchen. The afternoon looms ahead, empty and boring. I text Angie.

What are you doing? Want to come over?

Immediately she replies.

Yeah babe. See you later.

Good. I hope she doesn't go on about Si all the time though. True to form, he didn't ask her out again. Angie was soooo disappointed.

'It's nothing personal. It's his thing,' Tug said to us one day when she was moping about. 'He collects dates like trophies.'

'I really thought he liked me,' she said mournfully.

'He does,' said Tug kindly. 'But he's on a mission. He wants to go out with every fit girl in the school.'

I'm fit!

'I hate him,' she said, but anyone could see she was lying. She'd go out with him tomorrow if he asked.

So would I.

No I wouldn't! I don't mean it. Really, I don't.

The front doorbell rings. That was quick! But it's not Angie, it's Mum, leaning against the doorbell, her arms full of bags. 'I can't reach my key,' she explains. 'Give us a hand with these, Gabby love, there are more in the car.'

Her cheeks are pink again but with effort this time, or pleasure. She looks as if she's bought the entire contents of Mothercare. She hasn't been out long enough to do this much shopping! I take the largest bags from her hands into the kitchen and dump them on the floor. She follows me in and drops more on the table. 'There,' she says and sits down heavily. 'I'm whacked!'

'Cup of tea?'

She nods. 'There's a good girl. Want to see what I've bought?'

'OK.'

'Put the kettle on first.'

She starts pulling out stuff from the bags. By the time

I turn around, the table's disappeared beneath a sea of baby paraphernalia.

There are three packs of washable nappies, made out of bamboo for goodness sake (it says so on the packet), and one set of disposable nappies (biodegradable, of course); a couple of towels with cute little hoods on them; a changing mat; a bouncing cradle with a vibrating bar (cool!); a car-seat; a carrying sling; packs of baby wipes; baby lotion, bath oil, shampoo, cotton buds, cotton wool balls, hairbrush and scissors; a digital thermometer; a baby alarm; cot sheets; a pack of tiny vests; more babygros (not quite so posh this time); a set of bibs; a plastic baby bath; a feeding set with microwave steriliser, bottles and brush; one weird-looking object with tubes and a motor; and two ENORMOUS nursing bras.

I pick things up and examine them, bewildered.

'Do you really need all this stuff for one tiny baby?'

She snorts. 'Oh, you'd be surprised what they can get through.'

I inspect the feeding set, bemused.

'I thought you've been banging on about how breast is best.'

'It is,' she says. 'But sometimes, if you want to go out and leave the baby, you need to be able to express your milk. That's what this is for.' She picks up the weird-looking object. 'It's a breast pump. You see, what you do is—'

'No, don't tell me,' I say, horrified. 'That is too gross for words.'

'You'll get used to it. It's perfectly natural you know.' She laughs. 'You should see your face!'

The door opens and Dad walks in. 'Any chance of a bite to eat round here?' he asks then comes to a halt when he sees all the stuff on the table. 'What the hell?' he says, and if Mum thought my face was funny, she should have been doubled over when she saw Dad's. 'What's all this?'

'It's for the baby,' I explain, rather unnecessarily in my opinion, because it's pretty self-evident, surely, but Dad looks as if he's about to combust.

'POSY!!!! HAVE YOU GONE COMPLETELY MAD?'

This comes out so loud Freddie comes running in from the lounge to see what's going on. Before Mum can open her mouth, Dad goes on. 'I *warned* you! I *told* you to go easy on spending at the moment. And now look what you've done! Gone and bought up the whole of Boots bloody baby department!'

'Mothercare,' I correct him, but he's not listening.

'I've only bought what we need,' says Mum, all the light gone out of her face. 'These are essentials, there's nothing big here. We've already got the pram and the cot, left over from Freddie.'

'We've got the flaming car-seat as well, up in the loft,' he shouts.

'They're different now!' she says urgently. 'They're rear-facing, it's a new safety thing. They're good value, honestly. They double up as carry chairs.'

'Well, we won't want this then, will we?' He picks up the bouncing cradle and thrusts it at Mum. She takes a step back. Freddie whimpers and I draw him close to me. Behind Dad I can see Felix crouching on the stairs, peering between the banisters. 'Or this!' he grabs the baby sling and pushes it in Mum's face. Her neck jerks back. Felix jumps up.

'STOP IT!' he yells. 'STOP IT, DAD!'

Dad spins around and for a second I'm scared, really scared, that he's going to grab hold of Felix and belt him, even though my father has never ever in his whole life laid a hand on any one of us. But his eyes close suddenly, then he takes a deep breath and says to Mum, in a funny, broken sort of voice, 'See? See what you've driven me to?' and he drops the sling on the floor and storms out of the front door.

And we all stand there like statues and no one has the chance to say a thing because straight away the bell goes and I hear a voice calling, 'Gabby! Gabby, are you there?' and I realize it's Angie.

'Coming!' I yell, but she's already in, appearing at the kitchen door with a frown on her face.

'Is your dad OK?' she asks. 'Only he just passed me on the way out and he looked a bit upset.'

'He's in a rush, he's late for something,' I lie.

'Ahh, look at all these,' she says, turning her attention to Mum's shopping. She picks up the vests. 'Aren't they sweet!'

'Yeah.' I steal a look at Mum. She's packing things back into bags silently. 'All right if Angie comes up to my bedroom, Mum?'

She nods.

'Actually,' says Angie, smiling mysteriously, 'I've got someone with me. Guess who I met on the way?'

A figure steps out from behind the door, smiling modestly.

It's Si.

In the end we go out for the afternoon. All of us. Not Mum, but everyone else. I didn't want Si to come up to my room for some reason, I mean I wasn't exactly expecting him and I wasn't sure what I'd left strewn around. Plus, I didn't want Dad coming home and having a go at me in front of the others, I mean he's so unpredictable at the moment you don't know what he'll do next. So I say, 'Shall we go to town?' and Angie looks a bit surprised but says, 'Yeah, all right,' then Felix asks, 'Can I come?' and I realize he wants to keep out of Dad's way too, so I go, 'Yeah, if you want.'

Then of course, Freddie wants to as well, just because he hates being left out, and I say, 'No way!' and he has a screaming fit and I protest, 'Mum, tell him!' but she rubs her forehead and says quietly, 'Actually, I wouldn't mind a lie-down, Gabby, I'm not feeling too good.'

'You go and put your feet up, Mrs Sheraton-Hogg!'

says Angie immediately, full of concern. 'Freddie can come with us.' And the next minute we're all drifting down the road together, a real mixed bunch, with Angie at the front, hand in hand with Freddie, then me and Si (who's looking a bit moody now as babysitting was not part of his grand plan for Saturday afternoon) and Felix trailing along behind us on his own.

After a while, Si points to Angie and Freddie and says, 'Shall we hold hands too?' and he grabs my hand, fooling about, just as Angie turns round to see what's going on.

'Idiot!' I shrug him off and Angie laughs at us uncertainly. 'Felix,' I say, turning round, 'stop lagging behind,' and he catches up with Si and me and walks in between us which suits me just fine even though Si doesn't look too happy about it. The thing is, I don't trust Si one bit, and I can't tell what he's up to but whatever it is, I don't want him doing it in front of Angie.

In the end we jump on the tube and go along the embankment because there's always something going on there. There's a troupe of guys doing a mixture of acrobatics and break-dancing and we stand and watch them for ages. They're brilliant. After a while they start pulling people in from the crowd and Si and Freddie have a go. Si's quite good at break-dancing and Freddie, show-off as he is, throws himself around like a rubber ball, completely fearless. The crowd loves him and he gets a huge round of applause.

'Well done, mate,' says Si slapping him on the back, when they come back to us together, red-faced and triumphant. He turns to Felix. 'Your turn next.'

'What?' says Felix and looks alarmed. I come to his rescue.

'Look,' I say, 'over there.'

One of those people pretending to be a statue, covered in white, is standing on a box painted to look like a plinth. It's a girl in a long gown, hair piled on her head, tall and elegant.

'She looks like one of your designs.'

He nods and wanders over to examine her closely, his eyes widening as a man places a coin on the mat before her and she bends gracefully to thank him, then resumes a new position. He stands there, mesmerized, as still as she is, not even moving when Freddie runs over and shouts, 'Boo!' in her face. Si laughs.

'Freddie!' I yell at him, furious. The girl doesn't budge. Embarrassed, I fish in my pocket for some change and hand it to Felix. He places it quietly on the mat and she moves, her arms stretching out towards Felix, and nods at him gravely, twice, then turns back to stone again.

'How does she do that?' he whispers.

'Keep so still? Practice, I suppose.'

'I wonder what she's thinking?'

'What a prat Freddie is, probably.'

Felix nods in agreement, serious as always. 'I expect so. You don't know though.' He sighs longingly. 'Imagine no one being able to tell what you're thinking.'

I gaze at him. I *never* know what he's thinking. I'm just not on the same wavelength as Felix. I don't know anyone who is.

'Are you coming?' asks Angie, materializing from nowhere. 'I think the boys are getting bored.'

I turn around. Freddie is making a nuisance of himself as usual, spinning around so fast he gets dizzy and collapses on the pavement. Si is sitting on the wall with his hands in his pockets, doing his mean, moody impression. I glance at Felix who's still staring transfixed at the girl.

'Come on, Fee, time to go.'

I think he'd have stayed there for ever.

'Want a burger?' Si asks me. I shake my head, not sure if he's asking just me or everyone, and he looks even more fed up. Freddie immediately decides he's starving to death, so he and Si go off in search of food. Angie, Felix and I have a look at the stalls while we're waiting. They're the usual mix of London tourist tat and second-hand books but there's one stall which is selling ethnic gear, clothes and jewellery and stuff, which is worth a look. I'm fishing round in my purse because I've decided to buy some of that black kohl to outline my eyes with when Angie suddenly digs me in the ribs.

'Not your birthday, is it?' she giggles.

I look up to see Felix handing over a fiver. The stall owner is stuffing a bright orange sarong into a brown paper bag for him.

'Felix!' I call over. 'If you're getting that for me, don't bother.'

'It's not for you,' he says, taking the bag from the bloke's hand.

'Well, Mum's not going to wear it,' I say. Not at the moment anyway, though, horror, she might do when the baby's born and she's got her normal (normal for her, that is) figure back!

'It's not for Mum either.'

'Who's it for then?'

'Me.'

'You can't wear that!'

'Why not?'

'Because Dad's going to go mad, that's why not!'

Felix looks worried for a minute then he shrugs. 'I'll wear it when he's not around.'

'Guess who we bumped into?' says Si. He's back with Freddie, who's got tomato ketchup on his chin and is sipping a Coke through a straw. Well done, Si, I'll have a high-as-a-kite kid brother now to put up with for the rest of the day. Behind him is Tug. Angie smiles and says, 'Hi, Tug!' looking at me meaningfully, and tucks her arm possessively through Si's.

She can't be serious. Does she honestly think there's going to be a foursome with Felix and Freddie around?

Yes, she does. We may have bumped into Tug by accident, but now she's going to milk the situation for all it's worth.

'What've you bought?' Tug asks Felix, indicating his bag.

My heart sinks. Felix takes the sarong out to show him.

'Who's that for?'

'Me.'

Tug's face is a picture.

Si lets out a yelp of laughter and grabs the sarong from his hands, wrapping it round his middle. He wriggles his hips suggestively. 'Like dressing up, do you?'

'Yes.' Felix is nothing but honest.

'Get you!' Si says in surprise and hastily removes the sarong from round his waist. He leers unpleasantly at Tug. 'Got names for people like him, haven't we?'

Tug is silent.

Angie tries to snatch the sarong from his hand but he holds it up out of her reach, laughing.

'That's mine,' says Felix quietly. Si sniggers.

I hate Si. I hate his sneering face. How could I have ever thought I liked him?

'What?' pipes up Freddie suddenly.

'Eh?'

'What names have you got?'

Si looks a bit caught out.

'Tell me,' insists Freddie.

'Tell him, Tug,' Si jeers.

Tug shakes his head. 'Leave it there, Si, he's only a kid.'

'I want to know!' says Freddie bossily.

'Shurrup.' Si's starting to look as if he wishes he hadn't begun this conversation. Freddie steps on his foot hard.

'Don't do that!'

'Tell me then!' He stamps on it this time.

'Ouch!' Si scowls and backs away. 'You're nuts, you are. And gay boy here.'

Freddie pulls back his leg and kicks him hard in the shin.

'Ow!' Si starts hopping about, holding his leg. 'Psycho! You're mad, both of you.'

'Stop it!' I command and pull Freddie away. 'Don't you dare!' I warn as he bends over to pick up a stone and I grab him fast.

'You coming?' Si says to Tug, but he shakes his head. Si glances at Angie but she looks as if she's about to burst into tears. Freddie wriggles in my grasp, desperate to take another kick at Si.

'Weirdos!' Si spits and chucks the sarong on the ground, turning away in disgust. Angie yells, 'Si?' but he disappears into the crowd.

'Good riddance,' I mutter. 'He didn't mean it.' I reach for Felix who is standing beside me as still as the statue herself and give him a squeeze.

'Yes he did,' pipes up Freddie. 'That's what the kids call him at school.'

'Do they?' I stare at Felix in horror.

'Yes,' he says simply. Then he adds, 'It's all right, Gabby, I'm used to it. They call me that all the time.'

I look up at Tug appalled. He bends down and picks up the sarong from the floor, dusts off the dirt, folds it up and hands it back to Felix.

'Well, if a sarong is good enough for David Beckham, it's good enough for you, mate.'

Felix takes it from him and his face breaks into a smile. Freddie starts running round like a maniac yelling, 'Beckham! Beckham! Beckham!' I turn to look at Angie, the picture of misery, and say, 'Home?' She nods and we walk back arm in arm along the embankment together in silence, to the underground, behind Tug who is somehow miraculously managing to keep Freddie in check while at the same time chatting with Felix.

And I wonder to myself, what on earth did I ever see in Si?

When I get home from school on Monday, I can hear chatting in the lounge. I poke my head in and see Mum's in there with a nurse so I duck back quickly but it's too late, I've been spotted.

'Gabby!' calls Mum. 'Come and meet Julia.'

'Hi,' I say reluctantly, still hoping I can slope off. No chance.

'Come on in so we can see you properly!' says Mum bossily. She's back to her usual form. When we got home on Saturday she was still in bed with a headache and Dad went out to get us fish and chips, because we were all starving, but Mum didn't eat a thing. Yesterday she seemed better and got up to cook us a Sunday roast but then Gran turned up and took one look at her and sent her back to bed for a rest.

'You're all perfectly capable of lending a hand round here, you know,' Gran had snapped, banging pots around in the kitchen. 'She shouldn't be waiting on you hand and foot like she does.' But then when Felix cut himself trying to peel potatoes and Freddie wanted to help with the pudding and dropped a carton of eggs on the floor, she shooed us all out of the kitchen and got on with it herself.

To be honest, I get the feeling it was Dad she was secretly mad at, not us, because at least we tried. Dad didn't even get out of bed till lunchtime.

Anyway, the rest must have done her good because today Mum's back to her bright and breezy self.

'This is my first-born,' she announces, smiling at me proudly, like she's the Queen and I'm Prince Charles. 'Going through the terrible teens,' she adds in a loud whisper. 'Julia is my midwife, Gabby. She's going to deliver your little sister,' she says, smiling with excitement as if Julia's about to produce the baby out of a hat any second.

'Hi, Gabrielle,' says Julia, who looks remarkably calm considering. 'Posy?' she says, consulting her notes, with a slight frown. 'Did you find out the sex of the baby then? There's no record of it here.'

'No, I didn't bother,' says Mum. 'I don't need to, I've always been right. Call it women's intuition.'

'It doesn't quite work like that!' says Julia, looking worried.

Mum laughs. 'I know that, dear, don't worry. It really

doesn't matter to me what it is.' Julia looks relieved. 'But trust me,' says Mum, patting her stomach, 'this is my little Clover. I'm never wrong.'

Julia doesn't look convinced but she says, 'Now you're perfectly sure that you want a home-birth?'

'Absolutely.'

Mum's as stubborn as a mule. Once she's set her mind on something, she never wavers.

Hence the new baby.

And hence the next question.

'Have you brought the information about the birthing pool?' asks Mum, her face alight. Julia fishes round in her case and produces a catalogue. On the front is a picture of a woman in a hexagonal paddling pool with high sides. She's kneeling up inside it, leaning against the edge, her head bent on her crossed arms, and she's got nothing on. She's half the size of Mum but you can see her belly is swollen with pregnancy.

Mum looks up. 'Isn't it lovely, Gabby?'

'No, it's grotesque.'

Julia looks at me sympathetically. 'It's not for everyone, it's just one option. It can make labour faster and easier.'

'Is the baby born in the water?'

'It can be, but it's often used just to help the mother through the second stage of labour. The water supports her, calms her.'

That'll be a first. Mum? Calm?

'Yeah, but if it is . . . how come the baby doesn't drown?'

'It won't breathe till it comes to the surface.' Her voice is steady and reassuring. 'It's very safe, Gabby.'

I stare again at the picture. 'It looks massive. Where are you going to put it?'

'In here,' says Mum.

'Here! You're going to give birth in the lounge?'

'Yes, why not?'

Why not? Where do I begin? I have a sudden vision of us all sitting round watching *EastEnders* while Mum squats and grunts beside us, naked in the birthing pool.

I feel sick.

'What about us?' I blurt out. Not really what I meant to say.

'You can get in too.'

'That's not funny!'

'I'm not being funny!' Mum stares at me earnestly. 'Partners or children can join the mother in the pool if they want!'

She can't be serious. I look at Julia for help. She nods imperceptibly.

'Do you really believe, for one minute, Dad and . . .' I'm about to say 'the rest of us', but you never know with Felix, and Freddie won't miss out on a thing, '. . . I would get into this pool with you while you're giving birth?'

Her face falls. Even Mum's imagination has its limitations.

'Perhaps not,' she sighs.

'As I said,' jumps in Julia, 'it's just one option. You might want to consider others, Posy. Not just a home-birth but a hospital confinement.'

Now she's talking.

'If anything should go wrong,' she continues, 'it's the safest place to be and they're so much more relaxed these days . . .'

Wrong? What could go wrong? Cold fingers of fear curl themselves around my heart.

'Just bear in mind, Posy,' she says, 'if your blood pressure rises any more, this won't be a choice you can make.'

Mum says nothing but her mouth tightens. My heart sinks. I know who's going to win this particular battle.

That night I have a nightmare.

We're all watching telly in the lounge. Felix is wearing his orange sarong. In the middle of the room, Mum is sitting in a paddling pool, but only her hair tied up in a topknot with her purple scarf is visible. The Gemstones are there too, drinking alcopops and dancing. The door opens and Tug walks in, followed by Angie and Si, hand in hand. When he sees Mum, Si's face lights up and he climbs into the pool with her, dragging Angie after him.

We all jump in then and have a riot, splashing each other, even Dad.

Suddenly I realize Mum's disappeared. All that remains of her is her purple scarf, floating on the surface. I dive down into the water which is as deep as a swimming pool but there's no sign of her. She's simply vanished without trace.

I wake up terrified, crying for my mum, but it's Felix who hears me sobbing and comes in to comfort me.

The following week the birthing pool is delivered.

I'm a bit miserable when I come home, it's been a funny day. There's something up with Angie, I know there is.

I think she blames me for her and Si splitting up. She thinks it's my fault. He hasn't bothered with her since the day we had a row on the embankment and he stormed off. He doesn't come near either of us now.

That's so stupid! They weren't even going out properly. They only had the one date to the cinema and, knowing Si, that's all they ever would have had.

But she might have a point, though not for the reason she thinks. *I* think he was coming on to *me* that day. I reckon he only came with her to my house because he wanted to see me. I'm not being big-headed but when he grabbed my hand when we were walking along, I don't think he was just fooling about. He'd come on to me before, hadn't he, in Gemma's party and at the cinema? And then there was the taxi ride home . . .

So many things I haven't told Angie.

But she's got nothing to worry about. I hate him now, ever since he was horrible to Felix. I can't believe I ever fancied him in the first place. He's a snake, a cold-blooded reptile, and he's certainly not worth grieving over. Angie's welcome to him.

Only that's not really true. I don't want Angie going with him either. She's too good for him.

Tell that to her though. She's going round looking as if she's in mourning, which I suppose she is in a way. Si's hanging round the Gemstones now. He's got his eyes on Jade apparently, according to Tug. She's next on his list.

So it's been a weird day and I'm glad to get home. I just want to chill out in front of the telly and watch some mindless game show till it's time for tea.

But there's a funny pummelling sound coming from the lounge as if someone's beating the living daylights out of someone else. I push the door open cautiously.

In the centre of the room where the coffee table used to be, a huge blue paddling pool is standing in pride of place. No, actually, it's more like a spa. I can see Freddie's head poking out over the top. His face is furrowed in concentration and he's wearing the boxing gloves Felix got for Christmas, untouched till now, and he's doing a sort of kneeling skip around inside it, shoulders hunched, pounding the sides.

Mum is laid out on the couch, feet up, munching her way through a packet of biscuits and watching him fondly.

'The birthing pool's arrived,' she announces unnecessarily.

Great.

I won't go into detail about what Dad has to say on the subject when he gets home, though I think it's true to say that it gave his blood pressure a bit of a rush. His eyes open wide and his eyebrows rise up so high they would have disappeared into his hairline if it hadn't already receded. I just have time to put my fingers in my ears before he launches into a heated tirade which I'm pretty sure involves money because certain extremely loud phrases penetrate my blocked ears like 'POSY! WHAT EVER WILL YOU THINK OF NEXT!' and 'STUPID ALTERNATIVE RUBBISH!' and 'CAN'T POSSIBLY AFFORD IT!' and 'WASTE OF ★★★★★★ MONEY!'

'I've only hired it!' she's saying when I think it's safe at last to take out my fingers. 'Look.' She hands him the invoice. Dad's face goes purple and it occurs to me he might be having a heart attack.

'You could have bought it outright for that!' he yelps, his voice cracking.

'I thought about it,' she says seriously. 'But it's not worth it. I don't suppose I'll be having any more.'

Dad collapses into his chair, defeated.

One thing about it, this birthing pool is more useful than it looks. When Freddie goes to bed, Felix takes up residence in it, lining it with his duvet then snuggling up inside with his sketch pad and pencils. It looks really cosy, like a room within a room. As Mum, Dad and I watch television over his head I suddenly remember how Felix, when he was little, used to empty out his toy box and sit inside it. Mum said he used to do the same when he went to playgroup and one Christmas Day, when he was three, he spent the whole time sitting in the cardboard box his trike came in.

Well, I suppose if you're inside a box, you're protected from the outside world, aren't you? It's peaceful and private. No one can get at you.

Bit like being in the womb, I suppose. Like Mum's new baby.

I should stay there, little Clover. You're much better off where you are.

Mum is enormous. I didn't realize women got to be as big as this in pregnancy. She's like a huge humpback whale and she's still got more than five weeks to go. It's gross, I'm never going to get pregnant. I don't like kids anyway, but seeing Mum waddling about with a bellyful of blubber has completely put me off ever having children of my own.

Even Angie who thinks the whole pregnancy/baby thing is something awesome and sublime has a shock when she sees her. She comes around to say goodbye before she goes off on holiday and brings with her a big bowl of Mimi's famous brown chicken stew and dumplings, still warm from the stove.

The whole blinking family are going home to Jamaica for Easter – Angie, her mum and stepdad, her little brother and sister, Mimi and Kelvin, plus numerous aunties and uncles and their kids. The flats will be empty.

I say 'home' but Angie's never set foot there before, she was born in England, her mum was too. But Mimi came over when she was a little girl back in the Fifties, so they all call it home. There's some big family celebration going on, the gathering of the clans.

I wish I was going with them.

Mum's in the kitchen, emptying the washing machine, when Angie arrives. It's the end of term. She takes the casserole dish from Angie gratefully.

'How kind,' she says and sniffs appreciatively. 'Thank your grandmother for me.' She's wearing huge, baggy trousers, the only ones she can get into now, and what looks like an enormous old sack, though I happen to know it came from 'Mammamia's', the designer maternity range. It's a wonder she can still get behind the wheel of the car, the size of her. Her hair is trailing down her neck in lank wisps, making a bid for freedom from the familiar topknot which is tipping alarmingly to the left. She looks a mess.

So does the kitchen, the worktops littered with piles of unwashed dishes waiting to be loaded into the dishwasher and crumbs from the open packets of cereal and biscuits where the boys have been helping themselves. Since the cleaner left, the house is a tip.

I see the kitchen through Angie's eyes and feel ashamed. Her place is always immaculate, with everything spick, span and standing to attention under Mimi's watchful eyes.

'Are you OK, Mrs Sheraton-Hogg?' asks Angie with concern. 'Let me do that for you.'

Mum straightens up and supports her back with both hands, making her stomach stick out even more. I can't bear to look at her. Angie bends over and pulls my dad's smalls out of the washer.

'Thanks, Angie,' says Mum, one hand moving to rub her forehead. 'Got a bit of a headache, that's all. Carting all this weight about, I expect.'

Yeah, and who's fault is that, may I ask? It's too late to be feeling sorry for yourself.

'Go and put your feet up!' orders Angie. 'I'll make us all a nice cup of tea when I've sorted these.'

Honestly, Angie does my head in when she goes into Mother Theresa mode. I mean, Mum asked to be the size of a killer whale, didn't she? No one *forced* her to become pregnant.

Dad certainly didn't, that's for sure.

Resentfully I snatch Dad's boxers from Angie's hands and say, '*I'll* sort this lot, *you* make the tea.'

'Your poor mum,' she says in a stage whisper as she fills the kettle. 'She's massive!'

'Doesn't everyone get that big?' I ask, not really paying attention to Angie as I try to sort out what can be tumble-dried and what can't. Most of the labels are washed out. In the end I stuff it all in the dryer.

'My mum didn't, not even on Bolton and he was huge. She had a baby belly, but she wasn't big all over.'

'Yeah, well my mum was big all over *before* she was pregnant.'

By the time I've crammed the dryer full of Sheraton-Hogg underwear *and* got Freddie a drink and a biscuit *and* loaded the dishwasher *and* wiped the worktops clean, Angie and Mum are sitting round the birthing pool, having a cup of tea and a tête-à-tête like a pair of old wives. Or a couple of witches round a cauldron, more like. All right for some! Actually, Mum looks better already, stretched out on the sofa with her feet up, her back nestled comfortably against plumped-up cushions, mug balanced on her enormous belly. I plonk myself down on the edge of the sofa by her feet and reach for my tea, leaning back against her legs with the mug in my hand.

'Careful,' she warns, drawing her foot away from me. I glance down and am shocked. Her ankle is so swollen it looks twice its usual size and the skin is taut and shiny.

'What's wrong with your foot?'

'It's just a bit puffy, that's all.'

'Is the other one the same?'

'I think so.' She pulls up her other trouser leg and

examines it. If anything, this one looks even worse, inflamed and distended. I press it gently and my fingers leave an imprint.

'Ouch,' says Mum, wincing. 'Don't touch it.'

You should go and see about that,' says Angie, looking concerned. 'It looks nasty.'

'Or give Julie a call,' I suggest, a bit put out by the way Angie seems to be taking charge. She's my mother, not hers.

'No,' says Mum, covering her legs back up. 'I'll wait for my appointment after Easter. They'll only tell me to rest, that's all they ever do.'

'I'm hungry!' whines Freddie, as his programme finishes. 'What's for tea?'

'Brown chicken stew!' Mum hauls herself to her feet. 'I'd better heat it up. Your father will be home soon.'

'I'm not eating stew!' complains Freddie, but Mum's not listening. She's learning at last. She should have ignored his whinges years ago. By the time Dad's arrived home and Mum's dishing up Mimi's delicious-smelling food, he's changed his mind and is sitting at the table, fork at the ready.

'I'm going to miss you!' I say as I see Angie out. She won't stay for supper, she's got to finish packing. I fling my arms around her neck, feeling her warm cheek pressed up against mine and her soft hair tickling my face. As I breathe in her familiar fresh, sweet smell, I feel a lump in my throat, like I'm going to cry.

'It won't be for long!' she says and hugs me back even tighter. 'I'll bring you back something nice, I promise. And something for the baby.'

'Have a great time!' I say, my voice breaking slightly. It's not that I'm jealous – though I am of course, who wouldn't want a holiday in the Caribbean? – but I don't want her to go. She keeps me sane, Angie – no one understands me like she does.

She pulls away and studies me closely, not fooled by the grin I've fixed to my face. 'I'll be back before you know it.' She pauses. 'Sorry I've been a bit grumpy lately, Gabs,' she adds quietly. 'You know how it is. Si and all that . . . I really liked him.'

'Yeah, I know . . .'

She shrugs. 'Ah well, wasn't to be. Looks as if he's moved on, anyway.'

I give a heavy, world-weary sigh. 'Men, hey? They're like chocolate or ice-cream. Nice at the time, but they don't last very long.'

She nods morosely. 'No, you're right.' She squeezes me again. 'Not like mates! Hey?' Her eyes glint with excitement. 'Maybe you'll have your new baby sister by the time I get back!'

'No way! It's not due for weeks and weeks.'

Angie puts on her I-know-more-than-you-do-on-this-subject face and shakes her head wisely. 'Sometimes they're early, you know, Gabby. They don't all go to full-term.' She looks anxious. 'Oh, I hope your mum does though. I really want to be around when the baby's born.'

'Do you?' I say in genuine astonishment, mentally adding Angie to the guest list for the already crowded birthing pool.

'You bet! So don't let her go into labour before I'm back. Promise?'

'I promise.' I giggle at Angie's earnestness. Since when did I ever have a say in anything my mother decides to do? Anyway, Angie's got nothing to fear on that score. I reckon Mum is going to be pregnant, like a huge waddling walrus, for eternity. She'll probably end up in the *Guinness Book of Records* for the longest pregnancy ever, just so that she can fulfil her function in life, which is to be a source of continual embarrassment to her eldest child.

At least, that's what I thought when I closed the door on Angie that night.

Just how wrong can you be?

I'm lying in bed, thinking about childbirth. On television, women always give birth in the middle of the night. One minute they're OK, then the next they're doubled up with pain and are rushed off to hospital by car or ambulance, lights flashing as they charge through red lights. Then, depending on how brave they are, they grit their teeth and grimace heroically, or moan and groan and scream a lot, but whatever they do, the outcome is the same, they eventually bear down (or is it bear up? No, that doesn't sound right), give a few almighty pushes and a baby slithers out head first (yuck, I hate that bit). Immediately, they make a remarkable recovery and cuddle it in their arms, saying how beautiful it is, all pain forgotten, while the baby's father beams at them both proudly.

I know Mum's not going to hospital, that would be far too sensible. I'm reminded daily by the presence of the flipping birthing pool, which, by the way, will have to be emptied of all the household rubbish before it's put to its proper use. Dad tosses his newspaper into it once he's finished reading it; Freddie sneaks his crusts in and any other bits he doesn't want to eat; Felix is still using it as a den; I've even seen Mum dropping things inside it while she's tidying up, then she forgets all about them. If anything's gone missing, chances are you'll find it in the birthing pool. Needless to say, my stupid history teacher didn't believe me when I tried to explain where my Victorians' project was, but Mum wrote a note and I got away with it. I'm going to miss that pool when it goes back.

But basically, I'm expecting Mum's labour to follow the same sort of pattern, minus the car dash to hospital that is. Oh, and I'm expecting it to be a whole lot wetter and a good deal more splashy and, being Mum, much, much louder, not just because she'll make a lot of noise herself (which she will) but also because I know she's sorted out her favourite Enya CDs to play during childbirth. Enya CDs involve lots of wailing.

Which is yet another reason not to be present. I intend to absent myself from the house and its immediate vicinity as soon as the latest Sheraton-Hogg decides to make its unwelcome arrival.

Only, at the moment, with Angie away on holiday,

there's nowhere to go and nothing to do. First day of the Easter holidays and I'm in bed wishing there was something to get up for. Normally I'd have to battle with Mum for a bit of freedom during the holidays because she wants to drag us all off together somewhere as a family, but she's too knackered to take us anywhere at the moment. I can hear the boys downstairs, voices raised, arguing over the computer, and Mum's voice, tired and flat-sounding, trying to sort it out. I turn over and bury my head under the pillow. I can't stand a fortnight of this.

'Are you going to wallow in your pit all day?'

I must have drifted off again because Gran's sharp voice jolts me to my senses. I groan and sit up. When did she turn up?

'Your mother could do with a hand downstairs.'

I thrust back my duvet and get sulkily to my feet.

'You're all going to have to help out a lot more around the house now, you know,' she grinds on.

'What are you telling me for? I'm the only one who does anything round here!' I protest, furious at being woken up and told off.

'Really? You could have fooled me!' Her gimlet eyes sweep around my room, taking in the discarded clothes, damp towels, coffee mugs and sandwich plates on the floor and the usual array of bottles, jars, brushes, combs, straighteners, make-up, jewellery and . . . stuff . . . that adorns every available surface.

'I wasn't expecting visitors this early!' I say frostily.

'Early!' she sniffs. 'It's nearly afternoon!'

Is it? I glance at my watch. Oops. What's it to her anyway? She's doing my head in, it's not her house. Mum doesn't go on at me about the state of my room, well not much anyway. I pull a jumper on over my pjs and go in search of breakfast.

Downstairs the boys, still in their pyjamas, have declared a temporary truce. Felix is watching telly, some awful talk show where people get their fifteen minutes of fame by screaming at their exes, and Freddie's playing on the computer, some noisy, unsuitable game which involves blitzing his victims to smithereens. Gran's right: the house is a tip.

I glance at Mum who's spilling over on the sofa again. Her face looks waxy and grey today and her hair is hanging limply round her shoulders. She's still in her nightie too. She smiles at me wanly. I can't believe she's the same person. This baby is draining all her energy. In some ways I'll be glad when it arrives at last and we're all back to normal.

I go in search of cereal. There are two empty boxes in the cupboard and an old packet of cornflakes no one wants. Thanks, bros. What is the point of putting empty boxes back in the cupboard? I toss them next to the overflowing kitchen bin, pour what's left of the cornflakes into a bowl and drown them in milk. They're soft and the milk tastes as if it's on the turn. It's not fair.

'Mu-um!' I yell. 'You need to go shopping!'

Mum appears, one hand pressed into the small of her back, the other supporting herself against the door frame as if she needs propping up. Her ankles are swollen over the sides of her slippers and now I notice her face is looking puffy too.

'There's no cereal! Or milk! Or bread!'

'Oh dear.' She rubs the centre of her forehead wearily. 'I'll get dressed in a minute and go and get some.'

'You need loads of stuff,' I point out. 'Not just food. We need toothpaste and shower gel; oh yeah, and we're nearly out of loo rolls. Can you get some air-freshener too? The bathroom stinks when Freddie's been in it.'

'*You* stink!' roars Freddie who's earwigging from the lounge. Then he adds, 'Get some crisps, Mum. And some of those chocolate biscuits!'

'And pizzas,' chips in Felix.

'And ice-cream!'

'And doughnuts!'

She sighs. 'Whatever happened to healthy eating? I'd

better do a big Tesco shop. Someone's going to have to give me a hand.'

There's a deathly silence from the lounge. I take a sudden interest in polishing off my cornflakes.

'I can't do it on my own you know,' persists Mum. 'How can I carry heavy bags like this?'

'I suppose I'll have to do it. Do you know, Pauline, you've ruined those children!' Gran appears behind Mum, glaring at me as if I'm personally responsible for all of Mum's shortcomings. I scowl back at her. 'Gabby can stay with the boys and they can all have a bit of a clear-up while we're out.'

'It's all right, Gran, I'll go with Mum.' Anything's better than trying to galvanize Felix and Freddie into housework. Gran would do a much better job than me. Then my heart sinks as I realize what I've got myself into. If anyone spots me going round the supermarket with my elephantine mother I'll die of embarrassment. Especially if she's wearing that awful sack. I wonder if it's too late to change my mind.

'Thanks, Gabby, you're a good girl,' says Mum and I know I have to go through with it. Maybe there won't be too many people about.

There are millions. The world and his wife are shopping for Easter. We have to wait ages to park and when we finally get inside it's like a motorway pile-up with the aisles jammed with people and trollies.

'Oh dear,' says Mum, looking a bit pale. 'I don't know if I can face this.'

'Well, it's this or starve,' I mutter. 'Come on, we're here now.' I heave a bag of spuds into the trolley. Honestly, Mum's hopeless, it's like she's in a world of her own. She used to be so in charge. If pregnancy sabotages your body and mulches your brain like this I am *never* going to have a baby.

We progress slowly around the aisles in our traffic jam and I pile in stuff that we usually get and throw in some more besides because I don't intend on coming here again for a while. Mum is surprisingly compliant, just letting me get on with it. It's stuffy and crowded and thoroughly unpleasant. Too late it occurs to me we could have done this online and I wonder why I hadn't thought of it before. Because Mum never does, I suppose. She always says shopping with children is important for social skills, they learn so much. Yeah, right. All I ever remember Freddie learning was that when he wanted sweets all he needed to do was have a dose of the screaming ad–dabs at the till and Mum would give in. He learnt *his* social skills all right.

At last the trolley is piled high. I don't think we've got room for any more.

'Do you need anything else?'

There's no answer.

'Mum?'

She's gripping the handle of the trolley so hard her knuckles are white. Her hands are swollen too.

'Mum?'

Her eyes are glassy and she's breathing heavily. Little beads of sweat have broken out on her upper lip.

I don't like it. There's something wrong.

'Mum? Are you OK?'

She nods but I know she isn't.

'I've got a blinding headache. I'll be all right when I get off my feet.'

'Look, go and sit in the car and wait for me. I'll get these.'

She looks at the queues for the tills and her eyes close momentarily. 'Are you sure?'

'Yeah, of course.'

She smiles gratefully and turns away. 'Hey, Mum!' A thought occurs to me. 'Don't forget to give me your card!'

'Here you are.' She fishes about in the back of her purse and hands it to me, reciting the pin so loud I reckon the whole store now knows her number. I see a few people exchanging amused smiles. What is she like? I know it anyway, we all do.

'Go!' I say. 'I won't be long.'

Without another word she moves off towards the door, pushing her way heavily through the crowds. What's wrong with people? Can't they see she's pregnant? Give her a bit of room, for goodness sake!

It's called Murphy's Law, isn't it? The one that says when you select a queue to stand in, you've chosen the one that takes the longest time. You've managed to stand behind the ones with the coupons, the ones who've forgotten something and dash off to get it, the ones who didn't know it was two for the price of one and want an assistant to go and fetch them another one. The woman behind me in the queue is going mental, growling under her breath. She's like a snappy little terrier.

'Why can't people be more organized?' she yelps at the top of her voice. 'I haven't got all day you know.'

At last it's my turn and I unload what looks like a year's shopping up on to the belt and reload it into plastic bags and I wonder how Mum can stand this week in, week out.

'One hundred and eighty-seven pounds and thirty-nine pence please.'

'Sorry?'

'One hundred and eight-seven pounds thirty-nine,' the girl on the till repeats in a bored voice. 'Place your card in the machine.'

Flip. Is that how much it costs to feed us? I do as I'm

told and tap in the pin number when I'm asked.

'Can you do it again, please?'

The woman behind me tuts and sighs. I do so, more carefully this time.

The cashier looks annoyed. 'Try again.'

'What?' I don't get it.

The terrier leans close and breathes down my neck. 'Two-two-seven-seven,' she barks. 'That's what your mother said.'

'I know!' I punch it in this time, determined to get it right.

'Sorry, your card has been declined.'

'It can't have!' I can feel the blood rushing to my face.

'Oh for goodness sake!' snarls the woman behind me. 'She must have given you the wrong number!'

Mum, you idiot!

But she didn't! I know it's right! What am I supposed to do now?

'I can go and check,' I say desperately. I want to get out of here as soon as possible but I can't just abandon all this shopping, we need it.

'It's too late,' says the cashier, glaring at me as if it's all my fault. She hands me back the card. 'It won't accept it now anyway. Have you got another card?'

'I'll go and get one!' I say. 'My mum's in the car.'

Behind me in the queue the woman groans. Someone

else says, 'What's happening now?' I can feel people shuffling about, watching, starting to grumble. Without waiting to hear more I dart towards the door, pursued by gasps of outrage. I feel as guilty as if I've just been caught helping myself from the till.

Outside I pause for a second, getting my bearings, trying to remember where we left the car in this huge car park. I've never been so mortified in my whole life AND I've got to go back in there and face that angry mob again. I am *so* angry with Mum, it's all her fault.

When I get to the car, would you believe it, she's fast asleep! I wrench the door open and yell, 'Mum!' but she takes no notice. *She's* snoring her head off while *I'm* about to get lynched. I shake her by the arm but she's dead to the world so, in fury, I grab her handbag and start rummaging through it for her purse. Lots more pieces of plastic in it but they're all store cards.

'Wake up!' I snap and she gives a little snort but takes no notice. How can she sleep as deeply as this in the middle of a busy car park? I look at her and my heart misses a beat. Her eyes, like slits in her swollen face, are not quite closed and there's a line of dribble coming down one side of her chin. Her face looks like a balloon. What's happened?

'Mum?'

No answer.

'MUM?!!' I scream and slap her face, her hands, but she just makes a funny sound, deep in her throat. I straighten up, banging my head hard on the top of the door, and look around for help. 'My mum . . .' I whimper, but the woman going past with a loaded trolley ignores me. 'Help me, help me, help me,' I moan, but no one is listening.

I don't know what to do. 'Mu-um,' I cry, tears rolling down my cheeks. She can't hear me.

'What's up, love?' A man stops beside me.

I grab him, terrified he's going to disappear. 'Mum,' I sob desperately. 'There's something wrong with my mum. She won't wake up.'

He elbows me aside and bends down to take a look at her through the open door. He presses his hand to the side of her throat then he looks up at me, his face full of concern.

'Have you got a mobile?' he asks.

I nod.

'Ring for an ambulance then. Quick as you can.'

So Mum was rushed to hospital in an ambulance after all.

I'm so scared, it's all a bit of a blur. Before I know it, she's hooked up to lines and drips and we're on our way, racing through the traffic, siren wailing. The paramedic keeps talking to her all the time, so gently, explaining what he's doing, but she doesn't respond. She's completely out of it. I want to ask him if she's going to die but I'm too scared. I keep staring at her feet because, I'm not kidding, they're the size of watermelons, and I think, they're going to burst, my mum's going to burst, and I start crying again, but the guy doesn't notice because he's too busy with Mum.

When we get there she's rushed away and I'm not allowed to go with her. I have to give our details at the desk then I'm told to sit in the waiting room with loads of others. There's a lot of coming and going, with names being called and people disappearing behind blue-curtained cubicles. After a while a nurse appears in front of me. She bends down on her haunches and places her hands on my arms. I'm terrified.

'Gabby?' she asks gently.

'Is she all right?' I sob.

'She's in good hands,' she says, which I know is not a proper answer, but is better than the one I was dreading. 'Who should I contact? Your dad?'

'He's at work. I haven't got the number. My gran's home though, with my brothers.'

She scribbles down the number and disappears. After a while she's back with a cup of tea.

'I've spoken to your gran and she's got hold of your dad. They're on their way. They'll be here as soon as they can. Here, drink this.' She sits down on the seat next to me.

The tea is hot and far too sweet but I sip it gratefully till it's all gone.

'Is that better?' The nurse takes the empty cup from my hands.

I nod. 'Mum would have a fit, all that sugar.' Her eyes soften and her hand reaches out to briefly cover mine. 'Can you find out what's happening, please?'

'I'll try. Look, I'm going to move you into a side room, you can wait in there till the doctor comes to see you.'

My eyes open wide with shock. I know what that means. I've been watching hospital dramas for years. She must've read my mind because she instantly jumps in with, 'Don't worry, it's just that you'll be more private and comfortable there. Come with me.'

I follow her into a little room lined with chairs, with a coffee table in the middle covered in magazines. I thumb through them, trying to keep my mind off what could be happening to Mum. They're years out of date and they're all boring, middle-aged women stuff, or specialist magazines on things like house design, health, country living or golf. Who wants to read this rubbish anyway?

Mum and Dad probably.

When's Dad going to get here?

In the end, I start reading an article about kids and the internet called 'Who is talking to your children?' Mum would be so into this. It's quite interesting actually. So, when Dad, Gran and the boys finally come in together, looking worried sick, I'm surprised to find I've calmed down a bit. Freddie runs straight to me and hugs me round the waist.

'Where's Mum?' he asks.

'What happened?' says Dad, crushing me to him. Felix sits down and picks up a magazine but I can tell he's listening. Gran sits next to him on the edge of the chair, her back ramrod straight, grasping her handbag tightly on her knees.

'I dunno. She collapsed, I guess. I didn't see it happen. She was unconscious, Dad. It was horrible.' I can feel myself welling up with tears again. Freddie lets out a wail.

'Where were you then?' Gran's voice is accusatory.

'In the shop paying. She was waiting in the car. It's still in Tesco's car park.'

'Don't worry. I'll pick it up later,' says Dad.

Suddenly, I remember. 'The debit card wouldn't work.'

'What?' Dad frowns. 'Are you sure?'

'Yes! I had to leave all the shopping and go and find Mum. Oh flip!' I have a sudden vision of the girl at the till still waiting for me to return, and the terrier woman, and a queue of irate shoppers stretching for miles behind my abandoned trolley. 'It's still there!'

'Never mind that,' says Gran. 'How's your mother?'

'I don't know. We've got to wait here for the doctor. They said they'd come and tell us when they had some news. It's been ages.'

'Leonard,' says Gran, her face looking stricken. 'Go and find out.'

Dad's gone a long time. When he comes back he's looks older somehow, greyer.

'She's in theatre. They're operating now.'

Gran gasps. Felix slides his hand into mine.

'What's she having an operation for? There's nothing wrong with her!' I know how stupid that sounds, I should know better, me more than anyone. I mean, I was with her, I know how dreadful she looked. But I'm struggling to understand. 'She's just pregnant, that's all.'

'She's having an emergency Caesarian.' He looks as if he's going to cry. 'That's all they'll tell me.'

'What's an emergency Caesarian?' asks Freddie but no one answers. For once in his life he doesn't keep on. Dad sits down with his head in his hands; Felix turns his face to the wall. Gran clenches her handbag even tighter.

'But the birthing pool . . . she wanted the birthing pool.' No one looks at me except for Freddie who comes over to me and sidles on to my lap. He's too big really. My arms go round him, nevertheless, and I press my cheek against his head.

'It's all gone wrong,' I mutter into his soft blond hair, so quietly no one can hear. 'It wasn't meant to be like this.'

Our baby brother is born at 2.44 p.m. on Good Friday afternoon by Caesarian section, five weeks too soon. He weighs just over two kilograms. About four and a half pounds. Not much more than two bags of sugar. Not much is it? My mother looked as if she was carrying two bags of cement. They whisk him off to the special care baby unit and put him in an incubator, but considering he's so early, they tell us, there's actually very little wrong with him. The good thing is, his lungs are already developed enough for him to breathe on his own. He's going to be all right.

We all troop down to the unit to see him. He's lying on his back with his eyes closed and he's wearing a funny little gauze hat. His head is not much bigger than a cooking apple and his eyelids are swollen and too large for his face. His arms and legs are skinny and he's wearing a nappy that looks much too big for him. His skin is mottled and baggy, like he needs to grow into it, and almost transparent. You can see blue veins in the side of his head.

A little green tube dangles out of the end of his nose.

'What's that for?' I ask in alarm.

'Nothing to worry about,' says the nurse. 'It's a feeding tube. Baby's not quite strong enough to suck straight from the breast yet.'

I swallow, dying to ask more questions, but too scared to hear the answers.

'He's tiny!' says Felix, awestruck.

'He's weird!' says Freddie.

'Poor little scrap!' says Gran.

Dad and I say nothing.

'What's his name?' asks Freddie.

We all look at one another.

'Clover,' says Felix.

'Don't be silly,' says Dad. 'We can't call a boy Clover.'

'Mum said he was going to be called Clover,' points out Felix, doggedly. 'I like it.'

'We are NOT calling him Clover,' snaps Dad, starting to get angry.

'Mum thought he was a girl, Fee,' I chip in, noticing the nurse looking alarmed as if she thinks World War Three is about to break out amongst her premature babies. 'Let's see what she wants, hey?'

But it's not as simple as that. When we finally get to see Mum she's flat on her back in a hospital bed, wired up to machines and drips, and she looks as though she's unconscious. We all fall silent when we see her lying there and I can feel those cold fingers of fear grabbing my heart again. But then she opens her eyes and smiles weakly at us and says, 'Well, we didn't expect this, did we?' and I relax. I can't see her feet but her face doesn't look swollen any more. She's really tired though, she keeps drifting off to sleep while we're talking, so she doesn't get round to telling us what she'd like the new baby to be called.

In fact, I don't think she mentions the new baby at all.

The doctor comes to talk to Dad. He says she had

something called pre-eclampsia. I'm not sure actually, she might have got proper eclampsia, it was quite hard to follow what the doctor was saying. He seemed a bit angry like he thought it should have been detected earlier. The way he was cross-examining Dad, you'd have thought it was his fault.

'Her blood pressure was sky-high. Did she not complain of headaches? Blurred vision?'

'Not that I know of,' says Dad.

'She did, Dad. She's had a headache for ages. This morning when we went to Tesco's, she said it was killing her.'

The doctor purses his lips. 'Intense headaches, sudden weight gain . . . they're classic symptoms of the condition.'

'She's always been heavy . . . it was hard to notice . . .' splutters Dad, as if he's trying to wriggle out of something.

The doctor gives him a look of dislike. 'She should have been on total bed rest. Both she and the baby were at risk.' He lowers his voice and I crane to hear. 'If we hadn't acted quickly this could have resulted in convulsions, coma . . . The consequences could have been fatal for both mother and child.'

I feel my heart leaping into my throat. Dad looks stunned.

'Is she going to be all right?' he asks.

The doctor pauses. I'm afraid to breathe.

'Yes,' he says finally. 'She should be fine. She's been very lucky.'

On the way home from the hospital, Gran says we should stop and get fish and chips. Dad doesn't want to but Gran insists.

'There's not much to feed them on at home, Leonard,' she says crossly. 'They haven't have any lunch and it's nearly bedtime.'

'I'm starving,' says Freddie predictably and gives a huge yawn. He looks more ready for bed than a good feed but he's not going to miss out.

'Gran's right, Dad,' I say. 'Mum and I were doing a big shop, remember, but we had to abandon it.'

'OK,' he says. 'Whatever.' I glance at him, amused, and he gives me a little wink. He looks exhausted.

'Can we have pizza?' asks Freddie quickly, trying it on, but Dad doesn't even bother to reply. Soon Freddie's asleep and the car is heavy with silence, the rest of us trying to take in the events of the day. At last, just before we reach home, Dad pulls into a chippie.

He gets out of the car and starts fishing about in his pocket, counting out coins carefully into his palm. Gran sniffs and dives into her handbag.

'Here!' she says, thrusting a twenty-pound note into

my hand. 'Fish and chips all round. My treat!'

Dad looks embarrassed.

'Go on!' she says bossily. 'It's a celebration. New baby and everything!'

'Thanks, Gran!' we chorus. Dad and I go into the shop together. I check the prices on the wall.

'Dad? I don't think I've got enough for five.'

'What?' He shoves his hand in his pocket and then changes his mind. 'It's all right, I don't want any. Just get enough for you lot.' He clears his throat. 'Have you got that debit card on you, Gabby?'

I give it to him. 'Doesn't work, you know.'

'I know.' He sighs deeply. 'I'll get on to the bank.' He walks back to the door and stands there looking out on the street, hands in pockets, shoulders hunched, while I wait in the queue.

He doesn't look like he's celebrating.

He looks defeated.

That night, after we've eaten, I coax Freddie into his pyjamas, make sure he's rattled his toothbrush round his teeth and bundle him into bed. When I come back downstairs, Felix has made a nest in the birthing pool amongst his duvet and pillows, and is busy drawing in his sketch pad. Dad is on the computer in his study. When he senses me watching him he says, 'Not now, Gabby, I'm busy.' He's checking his bank statement.

I peep into the kitchen where Gran is tackling a huge pile of ironing. There's a lot of hissing and spitting as she bangs the iron around ferociously, pressing the clothes into instant submission. I back away quickly before she turns her attention to me.

Upstairs I throw myself on my bed. I wish Angie was around. It's been one of the most dramatic days of my life. My mother nearly died and I've got a brand-new baby brother and there's no one to tell. Hurry back, Angie, please.

As if on cue, my mobile rings. I pick it up eagerly, convinced for a second it's her, phoning from Jamaica.

'Angie?'

There's silence, then a puzzled voice says, 'I thought she was in the Caribbean?'

It's Gemma. I control the sigh that threatens to engulf me. At least it's someone to talk to.

'What have you been up to?' she continues.

'You're never going to believe this . . . !' I begin and settle down comfortably on my bed to tell her the whole, incredible tale.

Mum and the baby stay in hospital for a while. Gran comes to look after us. It's not so bad. She's much more organized than Mum and soon starts licking the house back into shape. The first thing to go is the birthing pool, much to Felix's disappointment. He's kind of declared ownership of it, making it into his own little hide-out. It takes ages for him to clear everything out. Gran makes me give him a hand.

'These are good, Fee!' He's done a series of sketches of the new baby, lying in his incubator on his back, like a little frog with splayed out arms and legs. I know, frogs don't have arms, but you know what I mean! It's not that the sketches look like him but Felix has sort of captured his essence, the *contradiction* of him, if you know what I mean. That strange, old man, other-world look he has, like ET, as if he's come from another planet but has been around for ages, combined with a terrible brand-new fragility as if he's too young and helpless to survive on this one.

'Freddie's right,' I say, studying them closely. 'He's weird.'

'He's an alien,' says Freddie, putting my thoughts into words exactly.

'No he isn't!' Felix snatches them back off me. 'He's not anything. He's just a baby who arrived too soon, that's all.'

Trust Felix. He accepts people without question. That's why he can't defend himself when people attack him. He's so non-judgemental. Not like me.

My phone rings. It's Gemma, again. She's been ringing quite a bit over the past few days. Gemma is not a bit like Felix. She's really critical of anyone who's not one of her gang. Except me, apparently. We've been getting on quite well, chatting on the phone. She's not so bad when it's just her. I think she gets a bit bored with Jade and the others sometimes.

Gemma blithers on for ages about herself, the Gemstones, Si, who she's still holding a torch for, herself again, then she says, 'You should come round with us, Gabby. We have a right laugh! Come out with us tomorrow.'

I hesitate, searching my brain for a suitable excuse. 'I don't know. It's difficult at the moment, what with Mum being in hospital. I'll have to ask Gran.'

It's not really true. Gran doesn't stop me going out at all, she just keeps me busy if I'm in. I'm wary of Gemma, that's the thing, I don't trust her, not when she's with the rest of the gang. They egg each other on to be stupid. Angie would go ballistic if she knew I was hanging out with them all.

But Angie's not here, is she? She's sunning herself in Jamaica, lucky thing, just when I need her. All right for some.

Gran's voice comes scraping from the kitchen.

'Gabrielle? Can you put this washing on the line for me, please? Then I need you to nip to the shop for me. You can take Freddie with you.'

'I don't want to go to the shop!' roars Freddie automatically. I make a swift decision.

'Yeah, Gemma, I'll come. What time?'

'Two o'clock at the station. Don't be late.'

We all go to visit Mum when Dad comes home from work. She's sitting up in bed and she's looking loads better. Next to her the baby, wearing a pink hat that's miles too big for him, is fast asleep in a Perspex cot.

'What's this?' says Dad, looking pleased. 'He's out of special care already?'

'Yes.' She looks at the baby. 'He's doing well, so they say.'

'Why's he wearing a pink hat?' I ask.

'I didn't have a blue one. He doesn't mind.'

Gran frowns. 'I've got some white wool. I'll knit him one tonight.'

The baby is lying on his back today, wrapped up in a blanket. He still looks extra-terrestrial. ET, in a pink woolly hat.

'Did we look like him?'

'No.' Mum smiles at me fondly. 'You were all beautiful babies.'

Thank goodness for that. I gaze at him in silence. Ugly little thing. Even your own mother doesn't think you're beautiful. Felix slips his hand into the cot and places a finger inside his fist. The baby stirs and curls his hand round Felix's finger, grasping it tight. Felix's face is a picture.

'He's holding me! Look!'

Freddie pushes me out of the way, he wants a go.

'Don't wake him!' cries Mum. 'It's taken me ages to settle him!' She shifts uncomfortably in the bed. 'He's feeding from me now. It's hard to hold him, I'm so sore. The nurse had to help me.' She strokes her belly. It's still really big. I thought it would've gone down immediately – I mean, she's had the baby after all.

I wonder what her scar's like? How many stitches has she got? I don't like to ask.

'Put him on the bottle,' says Gran. 'Never did you any harm.'

Mum looks annoyed. 'You know I wouldn't do that, Mum,' she says. 'Breast is best. I fed all the others and I'll feed him.'

I suddenly have a flashback. Do you know, I think I can dimly remember my mother breast-feeding Freddie. It seemed to go on for years. I'm sure he was running around by the time she stopped.

I'll never be able to have my friends round again, not with my mother flashing her boobs at every opportunity. Gran must have seen the look of horror on my face because she rolls her eyes at me, like we're in league against my mum. I feel disloyal then and I don't want to feel like this, not since I thought I'd nearly lost her, so I change the subject.

'What are we going to call him, Mum?'

She shrugs. 'I don't know. We can't call him Clover, that's for sure.' Felix looks disappointed. 'I was positive he was going to be a girl,' she says pensively. 'Ah, well. What do you think then?'

'Colin,' says Gran. 'I've always liked Colin. Or Brian.'

I wrinkle up my nose. 'Si,' I suggest, then immediately regret it. I forgot I don't like Si any more.

'Rambo!' cries Freddie, after one of his heroes. 'Or Rocky!'

'I still like Clover,' says Felix quietly, gently stroking the baby's hand with his thumb, his finger still grasped firmly in his fist. Dad looks at him in alarm.

'Henry,' Dad says decisively. 'That's a good strong name. We'll call him Henry, after my father.'

'All right,' says Mum, sighing. 'Henry it is.'

We all contemplate Henry in his outsize pink hat. His little face screws up into even more wrinkles and his mouth opens in protest. A screechy little sound like a cat's mewl comes out.

'I don't think he likes it,' says Felix.

'Suits him if you ask me,' says Gran approvingly. 'Henry the Eighth.'

I try to work out Gran's logic but fail. Felix leans over the cot, stroking Henry's scrawny chicken neck.

'I'm going to call him Hen,' he says lovingly.

Probably the best suggestion anyone's made so far if you ask me.

Now I've got one brother named after a cat and another one named after a chicken.

The next day I go off to meet the Gemstones at the station, glad to escape from the house. I feel like a deserter from the War on Dust. Gran's having a cleaning campaign, battling her way through every single room brandishing the hoover like a Kalashnikov. Honestly, I'm with Mum on this; a bit of good, organic dirt never hurt anyone. I leave her on her hands and knees scrubbing the kitchen floor, muttering words to herself like 'germs' and 'baby' and 'disgrace'. Felix and Freddie plead to come with me but I say, 'No way!' and slip out quickly. I reckon Dad's got it right, escaping to work all day.

They're already there, dressed up to the nines in high neck tops and smart jackets. Luckily, I've glammed myself up a bit too. Gemma flings her arms around my neck as if I'm her best friend.

'Gabby, you look great! Fancy coming up to town? Do a bit of shopping?'

'Yeah, all right,' I say uncertainly, mentally checking my finances. I should have enough for the train, though I don't know if I'll have much to spend when I get there. Everyone always assumes I'm rolling in it just because we live in a nice house and I speak intelligibly. But I don't have an allowance or anything. Mum's the one who gives me the handouts if I go anywhere. With just Dad around, I'm not as flush as usual.

'Don't worry, I'm loaded,' says Gemma, like she can read my mind. She tucks her arm into mine. On the train they're loud, excited, discussing what they want to get at the tops of their voices. It sounds like a serious shopping trip if you ask me. They've got like an A-list of must-haves. I'm beginning to wish I hadn't come.

'What are you after, Gabby?' asks Pearl.

'Nothing much,' I say. 'Just some sunglasses I think.' They stare at me, unimpressed. 'Maybe a bikini for the summer,' I add quickly, trying to work out how much I've got left in my purse.

When we get to Oxford Street we hit the shops. Now the Gemstones quieten down a bit and weave in and out of shops in formation, checking out the collections with a concentration that would leave our teachers amazed. Occasionally someone buys something and everyone gets excited again. Jade splurges out on a silver metallic bag, Pearl gets some shoes with impossibly high heels, Ruby treats herself to a great jacket with lots of oohing and aahing and shrieks of approval.

We're in a big department store and I've checked the price on a pair of sunglasses and am on my way to the till when Gemma says quietly, 'Don't get those yet. We'll go for stuff like that in a minute,' and I stare at her in surprise then obediently put them back on the stand. I didn't realize there was a system to shopping. It's all very focused, very deliberate, so different from the haphazard way Angie and I shop.

'Right then,' says Gemma and they all gather round. 'What we going for in here?'

'Skinny jeans,' says Pearl.

Gemma shakes her head. 'Tags,' she says, enigmatically. Pearl looks disappointed. What does she mean? Does Gemma make all the decisions about what people wear?

'Those vest tops?' asks Ruby, indicating a nearby stand.

Gemma walks over and inspects one closely. When she comes back she says, 'They're fine,' and everyone looks pleased except for Pearl who still looks a bit put out.

'Well, I'm definitely going to get one of those necklaces,' Pearl says.

'What the star ones? Me too,' says Jade. They both look at Gemma.

'Cool,' she says and they grin delightedly.

'I wouldn't mind a leather belt as well, to go with my new black skirt,' says Pearl.

Gemma wrinkles her nose. 'Dodgy,' she says. 'We'll see. Oh yeah,' she turns and smiles at me, 'and we mustn't forget Gabby's sunglasses. I think I might get a pair of those myself, Gab, if it's all the same to you.'

'Yeah, of course.' I'm just relieved she approves of what I'm buying. I can't wait to tell Angie about this. No one buys anything unless Gemma agrees. Weird.

'Right then.' Gemma springs into action. 'Colours for vest tops?'

'White.'

'Black.'

'OK. Do you want one, Gabby?'

I shake my head. They're nice but I can't afford one.

'On me,' Gemma prompts. I stare at her in surprise. Jade sniggers. I feel uncomfortable. Is Gemma going to buy everyone something? Is that why she makes all the decisions? She did say she was loaded. But I don't want her buying me stuff, I don't want to be beholden to her.

'No, it's OK.'

She shrugs. 'Suit yourself. Makes things easier, anyway.'

Without speaking, she and Ruby go over to the stand where the vest tops are hanging. She picks up a black one and a white one and takes them to the till. A minute later she's paid for them and she and Ruby are walking out of the shop together, chatting, the carrier bag swinging from her hand.

'Where are they going?' I ask, bewildered.

'Never mind,' says Jade curtly. 'We've got some shopping to do.'

I follow her and Pearl around the shop as they browse. They pick up the necklaces they like and examine them. Pearl lingers over the belts, running her fingers down them lovingly.

'Better not,' says Jade. Pearl's face falls then she picks one up anyway. After a minute, almost at random, they go over to the racks of jeans and grab a pair each. I notice they're each carrying a necklace. Pearl turns to me.

'Do you want to try anything on, Gabby?'

'Um, yeah, might as well.' I select a pair of skinny jeans and follow them into the communal changing rooms. I'm squeezing myself into them when Gemma comes back carrying her bag and two more vest tops on hangers.

'Thought I'd find you in here,' she says.

'Where's Ruby?' I ask.

'Gone for a coffee while she waits for us,' says Gemma. 'Want a top to try on with those jeans?' She pulls one off the hanger and chucks it to me.

'Thanks.' I pull it on over my head and stand sideways, admiring myself in the mirror. Not bad. I look at the price tag on the top and have to stop myself gasping out loud. They must be rolling in it if they can afford these tops. I'm surprised; I mean I know Gemma's well-off, but Ruby isn't.

'Wish you'd got one now when Gemma was offering?' jeers Jade. She's trying the other one on, I notice. It doesn't look as good on her. She's put the star necklace on too.

'Nah, it doesn't suit me,' I lie. 'I like the jeans though.'

'Me too,' says Pearl. 'Are you going to get them?'

I shake my head regretfully.

'I think I might then. Can I try them on?'

'If you want.'

I peel them off and put my own clothes back on. By the time I'm dressed Pearl's wearing the jeans and the top and they look sensational.

'Think I'll try the belt on with them,' she says and starts threading it through the loops. 'Would you believe it!' she says in a silly stilted voice. 'The price tag's in the way!' She dives into her handbag and pulls out a pair of scissors, snipping it off and doing the belt up. 'There!' she says triumphantly and swizzles round to admire herself in the mirror. 'Nice, yeah?'

Honestly, Pearl's got such a cheek. Fancy cutting the price tag off! She'll get told off by the assistant when she hands it back.

She's not going to hand it back though. 'I like it!' she says decisively, posing in the mirror, her hands on her hips. She remembers the necklace she's brought in and puts that on too. 'There you go,' she grins, twirling in front of the mirror, 'a whole new outfit!'

'You're chancing it!' says Gemma disapprovingly. I wonder what she means.

'Just watch me,' laughs Pearl. She pulls off the top and chucks it at Gemma. 'Thanks, Doll,' she says and takes the jeans off, putting them back on the hanger.

'You've left the belt on them,' I point out. Pearl stares at me fixedly and says, 'Duh!' as if I'm the stupid one, not her. I can feel myself colouring up. That's the last time I try to be helpful.

I sit down next to Gemma on the floor while we wait for the others to get dressed. She takes out a pair of sunglasses from the bag and says, 'Got your scissors, Pearl?' Pearl passes them to her and Gemma snips off the price tag and places them on top of her head.

'When did you buy those?' I ask.

'On the way in,' she says coolly. Pearl giggles as if she knows something I don't. I really don't like her, I've decided. Gemma pulls another pair out of the bag and hands them to me. 'I got a pair for you too. Are these the ones you wanted?'

I examine them closely. 'No,' I say. 'Can I change them at the till?'

Pearl chokes. Gemma ignores her. 'No, it's all right,' she says and takes them off me. 'We'll just leave them here.' She puts them down on a stool.

'But you paid for those . . .' I stutter. I've seen the price tag and I know how much they were. Pearl and Jade stand there smirking at me. I wish I hadn't come.

'No problem,' says Gemma. 'Come on. Let's go and pay for this lot.'

'Don't forget these,' says Jade and picks up the vest tops she and Pearl have tried on with the jeans, the ones Gemma brought into the changing rooms on hangers. I go out first so I'm not absolutely sure, but I could've sworn Gemma slipped them straight into the bag.

Outside the changing rooms, Jade and Pearl hand their jeans back to the assistant and Pearl goes up to pay for the jeans I brought in. The belt is still on them but I'm not going to risk pointing it out again to Pearl and be laughed at.

Anyway, I'm standing next to her when the assistant puts them through and she says, 'This belt doesn't belong to these jeans,' and Pearl goes, 'Doesn't it?' all innocently. The assistant looks at her suspiciously and I don't blame her. She puts them through separately and the price comes up.

Pearl says, 'Oh, is it that much? I thought the belt came with the jeans. I don't want them now.'

I know she's lying and so does the assistant, but she can't do anything about it. I'm so embarrassed I can feel my cheeks flaming.

I turn around, waiting for Gemma to pay for the vest tops, but there's no sign of her or Jade. Suddenly the penny drops. She put them straight in her bag, didn't she? They've been nicking stuff and I, stupid as I am, didn't have a clue what they were up to.

But the next minute, I have the shock of my life: Gemma and Jade appear, and they're being escorted by two big guys in navy blue tops and trousers, carrying radios. One of them has Gemma's store bag in his hand. He dumps it on the desk.

'Should be in here,' he says bluntly.

My heart drops. I know what he's talking about. The vest tops. I *knew* I'd seen Gemma drop them into the bag. Now she's going to get us all into trouble.

Gemma looks remarkably calm, though Jade's not as cool. She plucks nervously at her top, and pulls it up, biting on it. Gemma gives her a hard look and she stops. A woman in a suit comes up to the desk, the manager I suppose. She opens the bag and peers inside.

'Did you pay for these garments, madam?' she asks. I feel sick.

Gemma doesn't flinch even though I know there are four vest tops in that bag and she only paid for two.

'Yes,' she says, eyeing her coolly. 'The receipt's in the bag.'

The woman takes out a white vest top, then a black one, and then pulls out a receipt. She checks the codes.

'She's right,' she says stiffly. She hands the bag back to Gemma who takes it with a supercilious smile on her face. I don't get it. There should be four tops in that bag, I saw her slip another two in with my own eyes. Where are the others?

'Do you mind if we check the rest of your shopping, ladies?'

We open our bags. One of the security guards rifles through my handbag. I can sense people watching. I feel like a criminal. The manager pulls out Jade's silver bag and Pearl's shoes and checks the receipts. 'Nothing here,' she says shortly. 'Sorry, ladies, we have to check.'

'Can't be too careful, can you?' says Gemma, sunglasses perched high upon her head, a touch of insolence in her tone. 'Come on, girls, let's go.'

She sweeps out of the shop with the rest of us in tow. I glance back and see the two security guards, the manager, the till assistant, the girl guarding the changing rooms, all in a huddle. The manager stares straight back at me with a look of disgust on her face. It's obvious she knows what we've been up to but there's nothing she can do.

I just said what *we've* been up to. But it wasn't me. *I'm* no thief.

I feel like one though. I've been tarred with the same brush. I'm *never* going in that shop, ever again.

'Tags,' she'd said.

They'd taken the stuff without electronic tags.

It's worse than I thought it was. The Gemstones didn't just get away with the vest tops. Pearl and Jade had pinched the star necklaces too. That's what the high-necked tops were for. They'd taken them into the changing rooms and tried them on and had conveniently forgotten to take them off again. They thought they were so clever. I remember seeing Jade plucking at her top at the till and wondering why she was so nervous. She's different now she's on the tube and on her way home. She's cackling her head off and flaunting the necklace like a trophy.

I could smack her arrogant face. I feel like dobbing them all in, they're so cocky now they've got away with it.

It's Gemma I'm mad at most. She tried to get me

involved, even though I didn't have a clue what was going on. Those sunglasses. She told me she'd paid for them. Idiot that I am, I believed her. If I'd accepted them and been caught, I'd have been done for shop-lifting.

She got away with it though, didn't she? She stuck hers on her head and walked out of the shop as cool as a cucumber. She's flashing them about now, boasting about it. They don't care who's listening. I turn my face away from them and gaze bitterly at my own reflection in the window. Idiot!

'One for you, one for you, one for you,' she says, doling out the vest tops. 'And one for me,' she adds with satisfaction, trying hers up against her for size. 'Nice these. You could've had one if you wanted, Gabby,' she remarks. I turn back to face her.

'I'm weird me. I actually prefer to pay for things I want.'

'Oo-er!' squeal the others and fall about laughing. Gemma glares at me. 'More fool you,' she says dourly.

'I don't get it anyway,' I say, genuinely perplexed. 'How did you do it?'

Gemma perks up. 'Simple,' she boasts. 'I bought the first two tops, walked out of the shop with Ruby, left them with her, took the empty bag and the receipt back into the shop and helped myself to two more. Easy when you know how.'

I shake my head. 'But you don't need to steal. You said yourself you were loaded.'

'We do it for the buzz, girl. We do it for the buzz,' chants Jade and shrieks with laughter.

Gemma's eyes narrow. 'It's not stealing. It's known as helping yourself.'

'Whatever!' I huddle down inside my coat and turn my back on them all. In the reflection I can see Gemma appraising me, coldly, challengingly. I close my eyes and try to blot her out.

She wanted me to think she was big but I don't and she knows it. I know her of old: she won't let this go now. She's mad at me for not going along with her little tricks.

I should have stayed well away from her in the first place.

Mum and the baby come home a few days later. The house is spick and span, buffed and polished to within an inch of its life by Gran. Felix is so sweet, he's hung pink and blue balloons all round the baby's cot and a huge banner over the front door with 'WELCOME HOME MUM AND HEN!' on it in big pink and blue letters.

'Boy or girl?' says the postman as he delivers a stack of cards.

'Boy!' says Dad emphatically. 'Henry.'

'Nice to be home,' smiles Mum as she tucks into Gran's home-made steak and kidney pie that evening. 'Decent food at last. I hardly ate a thing in hospital.' She doesn't look as if she's been starving herself. Dad whisks a bottle of champagne out of the fridge and opens it with a flourish and she holds out her glass to catch it. 'Nice to be able to have a drink again too.' She takes a sip. 'Though I must remember I'm breast-feeding.'

As if on cue, Henry starts squawking like a baby bird. Mum sighs.

'Finish your dinner,' says Gran, 'he'll go back to sleep.' But he doesn't so Mum gets up from the table and bends over the pram to pick him up, hoisting him high on to her shoulder. He snuffles into her neck, then lifts his head to peer blindly about his new home like a little mole. His red face furrows as if he's not too impressed. He nods once or twice then his head bangs back down against her as if it's too heavy for his neck to support and he squawks again, more loudly this time.

'Who does he look like?' asks Gran.

'Dad,' says Felix. Got it in one! 'Only he's got more hair!' he adds.

We all laugh, even Dad. Henry obviously gets the hump at this because he starts squealing in earnest, his head waving about alarmingly as he roots around, mouth open.

'He wants feeding, that baby,' says Gran.

'I've only just fed him.' Mum jigs him about and pats his back. Henry's head bobs about even more wildly and he wails in protest.

'That's a hungry cry, that is,' says Gran. How can she tell? They all sound the same to me. If you ask me he's crying because he thinks his head's about to fall off.

'I'd better feed him again,' says Mum reluctantly.

Gran sniffs. 'Put him on the bottle!' she says. 'Then you'll know he's getting enough.'

'No, I don't want to. Mother's milk is best.' I feel a bit queasy. Cows give milk, not humans. Mum makes for the stairs. 'Actually, I'm feeling whacked. I think I'll give him a feed in my bedroom and put him down for the night.'

Too optimistic, Mum. He's still yelling when I go to bed and he keeps me awake half the night with his bleating.

In the morning everyone sleeps in, even Gran, as we've all been serenaded throughout the night by our new resident week-old Pavarotti. When I go downstairs to get a drink I'm surprised to see Dad snoring his head off on the sofa with his coat over him. His mouth is hanging open and he could do with a shave. He looks like a tramp on a park bench. I shake him by the shoulder.

'Dad? Dad! Shouldn't you be at work?'

'What?' He comes to with a jolt and sits bolt

upright, rubbing his face, then he slides back down again, pulling his coat back over him. 'What time is it?' he asks, indistinctly.

'It's gone ten. Where's Gran?'

He groans and throws the coat off, dragging himself upright into sitting position. He scratches his stomach and yawns.

'Make us a cup of tea, Gabby,' he mumbles, 'and take one up to your gran.'

I fill the kettle. 'Shall I make one for Mum too?'

He shakes his head. 'No, don't disturb her. The baby was awake most of the night.'

'I know,' I say, with feeling. 'Aren't you going to work today?'

He glances at his watch. 'Good grief, is that the time?' He sighs. 'I suppose I'd better get a move on.' He doesn't look very keen. Something occurs to me.

'Hey, Dad? Shouldn't you be on paternity leave?'

He looks at me blankly. 'Paternity leave,' he repeats, 'I should be on paternity leave.' He laughs, a short, bitter bark of a laugh. 'Well, what do you know?'

I turn away and busy myself making the tea. What's so funny about that? It's a statutory obligation, we did it in life skills. He should know all about it.

He's weird, my father. My whole family's weird. Thank goodness I can count on Gran.

★ ★ ★

Only, I can't. Not today. When I knock at her door with a cup of tea, a little voice croaks, 'Come in,' followed by an explosion of coughing. She's sitting up in bed spluttering into a handkerchief and she holds her hand up warningly.

'Don't come too close,' she rasps. 'I think I've gone down with a cold.'

She looks like she's gone down with double-pneumonia. Her face is pale and her eyes are red and streaming. I place the mug on her bedside table and back away quickly. She coughs again, an awful hacking sound, then rubs her ribs and says, 'Ouch!'

'Shall I get the doctor?' I ask.

Gran shakes her head. 'No, I've got some cough medicine at home, that should do the trick. A couple of days and I'll be as right as rain. Only, the thing is,' she stops for a moment, her body racked by another series of coughs, 'I don't think I should be around the baby like this, not with him being so new. I think I should go home.'

My heart sinks. I like it when Gran's around. She stops the house from descending into chaos. She can tell what I'm thinking because she frets, 'Perhaps I'll be all right. I don't want to leave you all in the lurch like this,' and I know I can easily change her mind.

But then I see her properly, struggling for breath and looking small and old and worried, and I have a sudden flashback to Mum, collapsed in the car, so I say firmly, 'That's all right, Gran, we'll manage. Dad's taking paternity leave,' and her face clears. I phone for a taxi there and then before either of us changes our minds and help her pack her bits and pieces. Before long the taxi's whisking her away to her bottle of medicine and her own quiet sick bed in her nice tidy flat and I'm left feeling very noble and very in charge.

Which lasts exactly five minutes. Just enough time for Freddie to wake up and throw a paddy because someone has finished off the Coco Pops overnight. He blames Felix, naturally. My money's on Dad, who's looking a bit guilty if you ask me, though he doesn't own up to it, coward that he is. Freddie grabs hold of Felix's sketchpad in rage and starts tearing his latest fashion collection out of it and Felix has convulsions and starts wailing like a banshee. Dad deals with it in the only way he knows how, and bellows at poor Felix.

At which point Henry wakes up, follows by example, and bawls his head off too.

Family life in the Sheraton–Hogg household. Bliss.

We muddle through for a while. The next day the health visitor turns up to check on Mum and the baby. Mum's expecting her. She dragged herself out of bed and got herself dressed and the baby fed and changed before she arrived. I noticed her gritting her teeth as he messed about at the breast but finally he got stuck in for a short while, before falling asleep, exhausted.

'Any problems with feeding, Mrs Sheraton-Hogg?' asks the health visitor.

'None at all,' says Mum. I look at her in surprise but Mum gives me a little frown so I keep my mouth shut.

'And how are you? Getting plenty of help?'

'I'm fine,' says Mum. 'My husband's taking paternity leave and my mother's here to lend a hand.'

My jaw drops open.

The health visitor doesn't notice. She's too busy writing up her notes in her book. 'That's good. Don't overdo it now,' she says kindly. 'You need plenty of rest.'

When she gets up to leave she turns to me. 'Look after your Mum, sweetheart. She's been through a lot.'

What's she telling me for? I was there, remember.

'Mum? Why did you lie to her?' I ask as soon as the door closes behind her.

Mum looks flustered. 'Lie? I didn't lie, Gabby.'

'Yes you did. You said Gran was around.'

'Well, she will be soon. She's only got a bit of a cold.'

'And you said you were having no trouble breast-feeding.'

'I'm not! I just fed him, didn't I?'

As if on cue, Henry starts to squawk. Mum looks at him wildly. 'Stop fussing, Gabby. You don't know anything about it. It's fine.'

The next minute I realize she's taken the health visitor at her word because she's disappeared upstairs to bed. I hear the bedroom door closing just as Henry lets out his first wail. I bend over and lift him up out of his pram and curse my mother softly in his ear.

There's so much more to running a household than I realized. Thank goodness it's still school holidays because I wouldn't want to be getting the boys off to school in the morning and washing school uniform and all that. I have definitely made up my mind I'm never getting married and having a family. I'd rather become a nun.

Which might be a good idea since I have no social life whatsoever and zilch chance of ever meeting anyone. With Angie out of the way and me keen to avoid the Gemstones there's no one to go round with. Anyway I'm too flipping busy making food and washing up and trying to impose some order on this house and the people in it to go anywhere. I might as well just sign up for the convent now, preferably for a silent order.

Dad's useless. He's supposed to be on paternity leave but he doesn't do anything paternal. Now I come to think of it, he never did do much, Mum did it all. When I ask him for money for disposable nappies you'd swear I'd requested a spare few grand to support my (non-existent) drug-habit, he's so outraged.

'Disposable nappies!' he splutters, like I'd asked for disposable syringes. 'I thought your mother bought those washable, organic, Tibetan flaming goats' wool ones? Save the planet, cost the earth, if I remember rightly!'

'They weren't made from goats' wool, they were made from bamboo,' points out Felix. 'They're more absorbent and they dry quicker.'

'What has she done with them?' asks Dad, looking around wildly as if he wants to strangle Felix with one.

'We've used them all.' I point to the festering black bag

in the corner of the kitchen full of soiled nappies. He goes ballistic.

'You're supposed to wash them, idiot! That's the point!'

'It's not my flipping job!' I yell back.

He starts pulling them out of the black bag to pile them into the washing machine and then discovers, like me (because I *have* tried to wash them but I'm not telling *him* that), that it's not quite as simple as you think. Most of them have disgusting things firmly attached to them.

'Gran emptied them down the loo first,' remarks Felix, helpfully.

Dad pauses. He pulls a tenner out of his pocket and thrusts it at me. 'Go and get some disposables!' he snaps.

Which is what I suggested in the first place.

Mum stays in bed a lot during the day because Henry keeps her awake all night. He doesn't seem to have worked out that you're supposed to sleep when it's dark. I rifle through Mum's baby books to see what's wrong with him.

'According to this book, newborn babies are supposed to sleep twenty hours out of twenty-four. Henry does it the other way round.'

'It's not his fault, he can't read,' says Felix.

'That's quite funny,' I say, but I don't think he's joking. He runs his finger gently down Henry's soft cheek and the baby's face turns towards him. He's not settled, even though he's been awake practically all night.

'Poor little Hen. Perhaps he's scared of the dark,' he says thoughtfully. 'I used to be.'

'I know,' I say, remembering. 'You used to get into bed with me.'

'Felix is a wuss,' says Freddie automatically, but he sidles up to sit on my knee and sticks his thumb in his mouth, looking at the pictures of contented babies feeding at their mothers' breasts with mild interest. 'I bet he's hungry,' he announces after a while. 'I can never get to sleep if I'm hungry. I bet he wants something proper to eat, not just silly milk from Mummy's boobs.'

'Do you know,' says Dad, popping his head through the door, 'I think I might go back to work. You guys seem to have everything here under control. What do you think, Gabby. Can you manage?'

I shrug. He doesn't *do* anything anyway.

'Right then. See you later.' He disappears quickly before anyone has a chance to object. I turn back to the book.

I think Freddie might have a point you know. Not that I think baby Hen should be tucking into sausage and chips just yet but I think he's hungry, all the time. He always seems to be rooting for food, like a little pig. If I pick him up and cuddle him, he latches on to my cheek and sucks like mad. Yesterday he leeched on to my neck and it looked like I had a love bite by the time I pulled him off.

I watch him: he's restless in his Moses basket, tiny fists waving about in the air, his little face screwing up as he gets ready to squall. His crying sets my teeth on edge, it's so insistent, like a shrieking baby seagull. Once he gets started, he never lets up.

'Time for a feed,' I say firmly and pick him up before he lets rip.

Upstairs I push open Mum's door. She's fast asleep. The room is in darkness and it's hot and stuffy. 'Mum?' There's no answer. I dump the baby on the bed and draw back the curtains. Mum lifts her head and peers at me.

'Gabby?'

'Henry wants feeding.'

'Oh dear. Already?' Her head falls back on the pillow. 'It doesn't seem two minutes since I last fed him.'

'That was hours ago. He's hungry, Mum.'

'Again!' She struggles up, wincing with pain. 'Ouch!' she says, rubbing her belly, 'I'm still sore from all those stitches.' She arranges herself more comfortably against the pillows and holds out her hands. 'Give him here then.'

I hand him to her. She holds him in the crook of her arm and looks down at him, expressionless. 'Are you going to do it properly this time?' she asks him, as if she's talking to an awkward adult, not a baby.

'What do you mean?'

'Oh he keeps fussing at the breast. He doesn't know what he wants. Here goes.' She grimaces as he latches on and starts sucking. Breast-feeding is not as gross as I thought it would be but Mum pulls a face. 'I don't think he's quite got the hang of this,' she mutters. Sure enough, a few seconds later, he stops sucking and falls asleep, mouth open. 'He's just messing about,' she says and looks cross. 'You take him, Gabby.'

'What am I supposed to do with him?'

'Give him to your father.'

'I can't, he's gone to work.'

'Has he?' She looks surprised. 'I thought he was taking time off.'

'He said he might as well go in, there was nothing for him to do here.'

'Did he now!' She looks angry but doesn't say anything. The baby opens his eyes and squawks again.

'He's still hungry, Mum.'

'No he's not. He doesn't want it. Here you are.' She dumps him unceremoniously in my arms. 'Look after him for me while I get dressed.'

'Are you going to make lunch for us? We're starving.'

'Yes,' she replies. 'Just give me a minute!'

She's so moody since she had this baby. What happened to lovely Posy who was so eager to please?

I take the baby back downstairs. He needs changing: he stinks and his babygro feels damp. I plonk him in his pram and nip up to the nursery to fetch a clean sleepsuit, ready for Mum to put on him when she gets up. There are none left in the drawer. In the corner there's a heap of used baby clothes for washing so I pull out the least grubby vest and Babygro I can find, scoop up the rest and take them all downstairs to dump in the washing machine. There's no sound from Mum's room.

Downstairs Henry is fussing in his pram; I don't blame him either, I'd cry if I had to lie about in smelly wet clothes all day. I locate the baby wipes under a pile of stuff and start to clean him up. It's disgusting, he doesn't half poo a lot for someone so tiny, it's everywhere. Mum should be doing this, it's her baby, not mine.

After I've managed to tape him into a clean nappy which is way too big for him by the way, I set about the business of changing his wet clothes. It's not easy. I'm afraid of snapping his arms or legs – they're like sticks – and he's not exactly co-operative. After a while, Felix comes in and watches me. I'm all fingers and thumbs.

'That vest is dirty,' he comments. I tug it over the baby's head which jerks alarmingly up and down over his little red body but then I have trouble matching up the pop fasteners on the Babygro. Henry, tired of being fussed with, starts to wail.

'At least it's dry,' I say shortly and press the fasteners into place any old how. Who cares anyway? Felix bends over Henry and sings to him softly. The baby quietens down as if he's listening.

'What's for lunch?' asks Freddie, appearing from nowhere. 'I'm starving.'

'Mum'll be down in a minute,' I say.

'I'm hungry *now*!' he whines.

I'm about to protest when I look at the clock and see that it's nearly three. No wonder he's starving. The baby starts to squawk again.

'Look,' I say, picking him up and dumping him in his pram. 'You two take him for a walk up and down the road and get him off to sleep and I'll organize some lunch.'

'No!' shouts Freddie. I take a family-sized bag of crisps from the cupboard and thrust it into his hands.

'YES!' I shout back. 'Or you get nothing else!'

When they've gone I yell, 'Mu-um?' up the stairs but there's no answer. I bet she's gone back to sleep, lazy thing. I want to go upstairs and pull her out of bed but instead I let rip a long list of all the rudest words I can think of and go and make some sandwiches. I never knew I could be so mature.

Food ready, I give them a call. Outside, Freddie is sitting on the kerb stuffing his face with crisps as the cars and lorries thunder past. Felix is leaning against the wall, hands in his pockets, still singing to himself. Next to him, above the roar of traffic, I can hear Henry's hungry wails emanating from the pram. I seize it by the handle and it moves. Felix has forgotten to put the brake on.

I glance up guiltily at Mum's bedroom but we're safe. Her curtains are closed again.

'Felix!' I say in exasperation. 'Put the brake on when you're not holding the pram.'

'Proper little mum, ain't she?'

I turn around. Gemma and Jade are behind me, grinning like a pair of Cheshire cats.

'Where did you come from?'

'Haven't seen much of you recently,' says Gemma. 'Thought we'd come and look you up.'

'I've been busy.' I'm curt.

Her grin slips. 'I can see that,' she says. 'Let's have a look then. What did you call him in the end?'

I pull the cover back to reveal a screaming baby, red-faced with anger. 'Henry,' I say reluctantly.

'Henry!' Jade cackles, then she adds quickly, 'Great name,' but you can tell she doesn't mean it.

'I wanted to call him Rambo,' says Freddie defensively. Jade splutters again. 'And Gabby wanted to call him Si.'

'*Did* she now?' says Gemma, her voice full of insinuation. '*That's* interesting.'

'*Isn't* it just!' says Jade, picking up on Gemma's tone. 'Who do you think he looks like, Gem?'

'Not like his mum,' says Gemma, pretending to consider. 'I think he looks like his dad.' They giggle annoyingly. It's not that funny.

'You don't even know what my father looks like.'

'No, but we know what Si looks like,' says Gemma, quick as a flash. Jade shrieks as if Gemma's said something hilarious.

Oh, I get it. The joke is, it's mine and Si's baby. Yeah right. I turn my back on them and call the boys. 'Come on, Freddie, Felix. Lunch is ready.'

'Freddie! Felix! Lunch is ready!' Jade parodies my accent. 'Makes a great mum, doesn't she?'

'Hmm,' agrees Gemma. 'Can't wait to tell Si.'

I turn back to face her. 'Get lost, Gemma,' I say clearly. Her supercilious smile slides off her face to be replaced by a cold, black scowl.

'I knew it,' she says menacingly. 'I always knew there was something up between you two.' She glares at me then turns on her heel. 'Come on, Jade. We've got mates to catch up with.'

I've done it now. I'll never hear the last of this.

I can't wait for Angie to come back from holiday. I *need* her. Gran's cold has turned to bronchitis and I'm running this house single-handed. Things couldn't be worse at home. Dad's never there and when he is he's like a bear with a sore head, picking on everyone, finding fault, moaning on and on about money. Felix is like a ghost flitting around the place, trying to keep out of everyone's way. Freddie is growing more and more objectionable as each day passes, but, funnily enough, I can't help feeling sorry for him. No one really notices him any more. He's gone from being the apple of Mum's eye to becoming practically invisible.

Actually, I think everyone's become invisible to Mum. She staggers around as if she's drunk with lack of sleep, not aware of anyone, not even Henry who cries all the time, a remorseless high-pitched scream that sets your nerves on edge, day and night. She's changed from hyper-mum to hypno-mum, as if she's been hypnotized. She's like a zombie.

And I'm doing everything!

But here's the strange thing. One morning the health visitor turned up at the door again and the old Mum came back.

'Is Mrs Sheraton-Hogg at home?' says the health visitor, standing there all neat and tidy with her bag in her hand. 'Only she hasn't turned up for any of the checks at the clinic and I wondered if everything was all right?'

I hesitate, reluctant to let her in because I know that a) Mum's still in bed and b) the house is in a dreadful state.

'Um, I think she's in the shower,' I say, trying not to open the door too wide. I can hear Henry screeching in his pram in the darkened lounge above the noise of the telly. She can too because she says decisively, 'That's all right, I don't mind waiting. I can see baby first,' and she steps inside, brushing past me, and heads straight for the screams.

'I'll tell her you're here,' I say and bolt for the stairs. She's going to see the messy lounge now and messy Henry too who hasn't been cleaned up yet this morning, or fed as far as I know.

'Mum! Mum!' I hiss, shaking her by the shoulder. 'Get up! The health visitor's here again.'

'Oh goodness,' she says, sitting up quicker than she has since Henry was born. 'Make her a cup of tea, Gabby, keep her happy. I'll be down in a sec.'

'Don't go back to sleep!' I warn, but she's out of bed and pulling on clothes as fast as she can, which is a first since the baby was born because she often doesn't get dressed now till Dad is due home.

'She won't be long,' I say downstairs in the lounge where the health visitor has Henry on her knee and is trying to examine him in the poor light. He's actually stopped crying, shocked into silence by this unusual degree of attention. Felix and Freddie, oblivious to the visitor in their midst, are watching the telly in their pyjamas. 'Would you like a drink?'

'No thank you. Has baby been fed and changed this morning?' Her tone is different this time, more concerned, more authoritative. She's not that old, definitely much younger than Mum, but she's taking charge. I don't know what to say. I mean, he hasn't, I know he hasn't, but if I tell her that I have a sudden feeling that she might whisk him away to a more suitable home.

And, I'm surprised to discover, I don't want her to do that.

'Oh my goodness, open those curtains!' Mum breezes into the lounge, making us all sit up in surprise. 'Switch off that television, Felix. You boys, go and get dressed this minute. What will this poor lady think of us all?'

The boys scarper obediently, taken aback by the return of Super Mum. She sweeps by to yank back the curtains and the lounge is flooded in sunshine. 'We're not normally like this you know,' she confides, lying through her teeth, 'but I'm afraid we've all had a lie-in this morning. School holidays, you know.'

The health visitor nods understandingly. 'How's it going?'

'Splendid!' says Mum, whisking Henry out of her arms 'Well, chaotic naturally, you know how it is with a family. Have you got children?'

The woman nods. 'Two.'

'Ah well then, you know what it's like. Still, we muddle through.' She holds Henry up to sniff at his nappy and wrinkles her nose. 'Pooh, you need changing, little man. Gabby, fetch me a nappy and the baby wipes, there's a good girl. We'll just top and tail him for now, he's due a feed. She's such a help you know . . .'

By the time I get back the two of them are chatting away like old friends with Henry on Mum's knee staring bemusedly into the distance. Minutes later he's been cleaned up and is having his first feed of the day at Mum's breast while the two women exchange stories of family life over a cup of tea.

I don't need to worry after all. The health visitor doesn't appear to have noticed the state of the lounge at all. She didn't seem to notice how Mum winced when she put Henry to her breast either. She was far too busy admiring the happy, smiling, family photographs on the mantelpiece.

If she only knew.

I am actually looking forward to going back to school for once in my life. I can't wait to see Angie and I like the summer term, when we get to play tennis which I'm good at on account of all the tennis lessons that Dad has forked out for me.

'I think I'll sign up for more tennis lessons at the club this summer,' I say that evening. 'Now I've got my new racket.'

We're all sitting down together for once as Mum stayed up when the health visitor left and made us a proper dinner. Not proper dinner as in pre-Henry days, when our meals were carefully planned and nutritionally balanced, though often, ironically, inedible; more like, what can I find in the fridge and create a meal from, proper dinner. But I'm not complaining, it's delicious. I never thought I'd say it but I'm sick to death of pizza. To be honest, sometimes, if Dad's not around, we've just made do with cereal or crisps.

'Yes,' says Mum. 'Good idea. Felix should have some too, ready for big school.'

Felix shrinks into his chair. I don't think he's ever going to be ready for 'big' school as Mum so quaintly calls it and the thought of physical exercise fills him with horror.

Dad clears his throat. 'I thought we might give them a miss this year.'

'Why?' I ask him, genuinely surprised. He's normally dead keen on us doing anything sporty, especially Felix.

'You don't want tennis lessons, do you, son?' he asks. Felix, who has never been consulted on what he wants in his life and can't believe his luck, says, 'No!' very emphatically.

'Well *I* do,' I say, just as emphatically.

'So do I!' chips in Freddie, never one to be left out.

Dad lays down his knife and fork and knits his hands together.

'Actually,' he says, 'that might not be possible.'

'Why not?'

'We can't afford it. It's an expensive year what with one thing and another. We've got a baby to think of now . . .'

'So *I* can't have tennis lessons because *you* wanted another baby! Thanks a bunch!'

'*I* wanted a baby . . . !' Dad looks as if he's struggling

to contain his temper. Mum looks down at her plate. 'It's not just that, Gabby,' he continues. 'Felix needs to go away to boarding school this year. I don't know how we're going to find the money for that.'

'I don't want to go to boarding school,' says Felix quietly.

'And I don't want you to either,' says Mum, looking up.

Dad frowns. 'Well, I'm sorry to inform you,' he says, going all pompous as he does when he's cross, 'but sometimes we have to do things we don't like. I didn't want to go to boarding school if you must know, but it didn't do me any harm. It'll make a man of you.'

'I don't want to be a man,' says Felix sulkily.

Dad explodes. 'You'll do as you're told!' he bawls. 'Your mother's namby-pambied you far too much. She's made a blooming sissy out of you!'

That is so unfair. Nobody's made Felix into anything. He's always been himself. But this is not the time to point this out.

The telephone rings. Mum gets up to answer it without a word. We kids sit there afraid to move. I hate it when Dad blows a fuse.

'It's for you, Leonard,' she says.

Dad hasn't finished yet. He gets up and jabs a finger into Felix's chest. 'It'll do you the world of good, young man! We're spending a fortune on you, so you just be blooming well grateful!'

Felix's eyes well up. Dad looks at him in disgust then snatches the phone off Mum.

'Yes!' he barks, then his face clears. 'Mr Babcock?' he says, his voice changing. Mr Babcock is Dad's boss. 'Yes, of course, sir. Nine o'clock? Certainly.' He nods once or twice and utters a few more, 'Yes, sirs,' then says, 'Thank you. Yes, I'll be there, on the dot,' and puts the phone down.

'He wants to see me in the office tomorrow morning, nine o'clock,' he says unnecessarily. All the rage has gone out of him.

He doesn't look like a big enormous bully any more.

He looks small and worried.

In fact, he looks like *he's* the one who's being pushed around.

At last the first day of the summer term arrives and I'm practically ecstatic with happiness. I've never been so pleased to go back to school in my life because, let's face it, it's been the worst holiday ever. Two weeks of running a house practically single-handed? I'm fourteen for pity's sake, not forty!

But today heralds a return to normal life. Back to school and back to Angie! She texted me late last night to tell me she was home. She wanted to come straight round to see me but her mother wouldn't let her.

I can't wait to see her, I've got so much to tell her. I didn't say anything about the baby, I wanted it be a surprise.

'Are you going to be all right, Mum?' I ask, shoving some sandwiches and an apple into my bag for lunch. I'm in a rush, I don't want to be late.

'I'll be fine,' she says. 'Don't worry about me.'

Mum's made an effort today, she's got up in time to get us all off to school, but she still looks tired and washed out.

'You can have a nice quiet day today,' I say, 'with all us lot out of the way.'

'Huh!' says Mum as Henry starts squalling from upstairs, right on cue. 'Fat chance of that with *him* around!'

I glance at her in surprise.

'I'll drop the boys off at school for you on my way to work,' offers Dad. 'Save you going out with the baby.'

I've forgotten how nice Dad can be when he wants to. Instead of making a fuss about how he's going to be late, he waits patiently while Mum searches for Felix's PE kit even though Felix explains he doesn't mind not doing PE if she can't find it, only he'll have to have a note. Finally Dad locates it himself, hidden beneath Felix's bed, and he doesn't even yell at him. When Freddie has a screaming fit because he *hates* cheese sandwiches, he wants jam instead, Dad just says, 'Life's not fair, is it, son?' and ruffles his hair and Freddie is so surprised he picks up his lunch box containing the said cheese sandwiches without further protest and follows him straight out to the car.

Maybe Mum was right, work was stressing him out. I think he must have got a promotion or something because that day when he was called into the office to see his boss, he didn't come home till really late and it was so obvious he'd been celebrating because he was out of his head, stumbling over his own feet and stinking of booze. Since then he seems less anxious about being in work at the crack of dawn and he comes home earlier too. I suppose you can do that when you're further up the ladder.

I practically fly to school, glad to be out without the encumbrances of prams and kid brothers. Angie's waiting at the school gate for me. When she spots me her eyes light up and we fall into each other's arms, hugging each other tightly, like we'll never ever let each other go again.

'You look fabulous!' I shriek. She does too. Her eyes and skin are glowing with health and she's got her hair woven into hundreds of tiny plaits threaded with the most gorgeous brightly-coloured beads in the shape of tiny butterflies. They're awesome.

'*You* look knackered!' she says. 'What have you been up to?'

'Don't ask!' I'm beside myself with happiness at having my best mate back. I knew I'd missed her but I hadn't realized just how much. 'You'll never guess what's happened while you've been away!'

'What?' Her face, split into a huge grin, is alive with excitement.

I suddenly remember her last words to me. 'I really

want to be around when the baby's born,' she'd said. 'Don't let your mum go into labour till I'm back.' And I'd promised! My face assumes a pretend mask of contrition.

'I've got something to tell you. Oh, don't be mad at me, Angie,' I plead, drawing out the whole performance, loving the drama of it all. Let's face it, Angie was the one and only person who would be genuinely excited by the prospect of my baby brother's arrival, so I might as well make the most of it. 'I'm sorry! There was nothing I could do to stop it!'

Her smile fades. She's taking me seriously! 'What is it, Gabby! What's been going on?' She grabs me by the arm. 'Tell me!'

I pause, trying to keep the suspense going as long as possible, but Angie's eyes are round with anxiety and I can't wait any more to tell her the whole dramatic story of Henry's premature arrival.

Then a voice rings out behind me.

'Confession time, hey, Gabby?'

I turn around. The Gemstones are standing there like a task force, ready to quell a riot. Only, of course, in their case, they're more intent on stirring one up. Gemma sneers. 'Going to tell your best mate what you've been up to while she's been sunning herself in the Caribbean?'

'And before that if you ask me,' says Jade.

'About nine months before,' retorts Gemma and they all snigger.

Angie looks at me, puzzled. 'What are they on about?'

'Nothing,' I say. 'Don't listen to them.'

'Nothing?' shrieks Gemma, 'I don't call that nothing, do you, girls?'

'While the cat's away . . .' intones Ruby,

'. . . the mouse will play,' completes Pearl in a silly voice.

'Out of sight . . .' Gemma picks up on the game,

'. . . out of mind,' concludes Jade and they all shriek with laughter. Angie frowns.

'Let's go,' I say to her. 'We need to talk.'

'You bet you do,' says Gemma spitefully, not laughing any more. 'Dear little Gabby thought she'd miss you, Angie, while you were away, but she managed to keep herself occupied.'

'Yeah, she kept herself busy all right,' adds Jade. I shake my head in disgust, fed up with them all.

'What are they saying?' Angie asks me.

'I'm trying to tell you,' I say, but Gemma's taunting voice interrupts again.

'I always thought there was something going on between Gabby and Si, didn't you, Jade?'

'Yeah, I did,' answers Jade. 'I reckon they were up to something at your Christmas party, Gem.'

Angie's jaw drops open.

Gemma smirks, delighted to see that her poisonous arrow has hit the target. 'Turns out we were right after all. There's no hiding the evidence now, that's for sure.'

'How's the baby, Gabby?' asks Jade innocently and they all shriek.

Angie turns to me, confused. 'What baby?'

I shake my head, furious they'd told her about Hen. I wanted to! They'd spoilt it now.

Angie stares at me then turns back to face them. 'What are you going on about?'

'Ask your friend Gabby. Come on girls.' The Gemstones fade away grinning, mission accomplished. Angie stares at me, her face confused.

'Don't listen to her Angie, she's winding you up.'

'What's she saying Gab?'

'She's being stupid. She's trying to make out I had a baby by Si when you were away.'

'What?' Angie's eyes bulge with shock.

'You heard her. She reckons I got off with him at her Christmas party.'

Angie gasps.

'Yeah right,' I say. 'That makes it the shortest pregnancy on record. How crazy is she?'

Angie laughs, a little uncertainly. Then she says, 'Why would she say that?'

217

'Because she hates me!' I say wildly. Angie looks at me perplexed and I realize she deserves a proper explanation. 'Because my mother had her baby while you were away and Gemma saw me out with the pram and she's a malicious, evil cow!'

'Your mum's had her baby?' Angie's struggling to take all this in. No wonder! 'Why didn't you tell me?'

'I was trying to!' I'm beside myself with fury. I didn't want to tell Angie like this. Gemma's ruined it all.

'What did she have?'

'A little boy.'

Angie is silent. After a while she says, 'What's he called?'

'Henry. He came early. He's tiny, Ange. You wait till you see him . . .'

The bell goes. I can feel the urge to batter Gemma's grinning face to pulp receding as I think how much Angie's going to love all this. I link my arm through hers as we make our way into the building.

'I've been trying to explain, Ange! My mum had the baby before Easter. She nearly had it in Tesco's! It was mental! You'll never guess what happened . . .'

By the time we get to the end of registration I've been told off three times and threatened with a detention by my form teacher but I've managed to tell Angie the whole account of Henry's birth. I knew she'd want to know everything in detail. It's great to get it all off my chest at last and I feel loads better after, because telling the story to Angie has made it sound funny instead of scary.

I'm really surprised though at the end of school. I thought Angie would want to come home with me and see the baby but she says she can't, she hasn't unpacked yet.

'So? Do it later.'

'No, I want to get home. I'm a bit tired. Maybe tomorrow?'

I stare at her in consternation. *A bit tired*? *Maybe tomorrow*? This can't be Angie speaking, my best mate? The one who made me promise not to let my mum go into labour while she was on holiday because she didn't want to miss the birth. She said she was going to bring the baby a present back from Jamaica. She said she was going to bring *me* one! She seems to have forgotten all about that now.

Maybe she's got jetlag.

She doesn't come round after school tomorrow. Or the next day. Or the one after that either. I didn't know jetlag lasted as long as that. I didn't know it made you quiet and withdrawn and not want to have a laugh any more. Or not answer your mobile or your best mate's texts.

I thought I was lonely when Angie was away.

I'm even lonelier now.

I wonder if this is what Felix feels like all the time? I don't think he's ever had a real friend.

I'm sitting on the floor of his bedroom and he's sketching me. He's taking ages and my legs are going to sleep so I'm looking at his latest collection to take my mind off them. He's designed some dresses for men. They're cool. I wonder why men don't wear dresses? Women wear trousers after all. I suppose Scotsmen wear kilts. Does that count?

I remember when Felix was little he went through a phase of dressing up in my clothes and good old liberal Posy let him get on with it. But then he started wanting to wear them to school, so in the end Mum dug out one of my old kilts and let him wear it. Then one day we had a letter home to say this was not appropriate clothing and Dad read it and went crazy, because, of course, he had no idea his son was going off to school each day dressed in an old tartan skirt. He yelled so much he went all red in the face and spit leapt from his mouth.

Felix never wore a kilt to school again.

I wonder why Dad won't let Felix be himself.

'Felix?' I ask. 'Who do you like best, Mum or Dad?'

'Mum, of course,' he answers, sketching deftly. 'Mum is much nicer than Dad. Dad's bad-tempered and shouts all the time.'

'No he doesn't,' I say, picking up another sketch pad and sifting through it. It's the one with pictures of Dad in it. In every one of them he's looking extremely bad-tempered. 'Well, not *all* the time.'

Felix doesn't look convinced.

'Ah well,' I add, trying to make a joke of it. 'That's men for you! Right nasty creatures.'

'Boys are the same,' says Felix. 'They can be nasty too.'

'So can girls,' I say feelingly.

Felix frowns. 'Keep still,' he says. 'I bet Leonardo da Vinci didn't have this trouble when he painted the Mona Lisa. I bet she didn't wriggle about all over the place.'

'I'm not wriggling,' I say, trying to ease one leg out from beneath the other without him noticing. I've got pins and needles. I watch him closely as he, in turn, studies me, his eyes focusing on my face objectively as he sketches swift, clear lines on the page. His face is rapt, blue eyes intent under his mop of dark hair, strong white teeth biting his lower lip with concentration. He's so good-looking, my brother. As Gran would say, he'll break a few hearts one day.

'Finished!' he says at last and signs his name with a flourish. 'What do you think?'

I study the picture before me. She looks like Felix, this girl, it could be a self-portrait. Same thick brown hair, clear eyes with heavy fringe of lashes, high cheek bones, straight nose, small, determined chin. She looks sad.

I wish she didn't. He's captured my mood.

'You're so good at this, Fee. You're gifted.'

'Thanks,' he says simply.

Why doesn't Dad notice what he *can* do instead of making him do things he can't?

What's your problem, Dad? You're worse than all those little kids who chase him and call him names.

What are you afraid of?

He's just Felix, that's all. Just Felix.

I'd been so looking forward to Angie coming home.

I was dying to tell her about all the bad things that had happened while she was away: Mum having the baby like that and how scary it was; Dad being so horrible and wanting to send Felix off to boarding school; that awful, shameful, shop-lifting incident which still makes me want to die of embarrassment. I'll never go in that store ever again.

I wanted to talk to her as well about something that was worrying at me like a nagging tooth. It was Mum. I was dreading this new baby arriving because I know how full-on she is about everything. I thought she'd be so immersed in the world of babies she'd try to drown us in it too with constant facile observations about feeding and bowel movements and child development that would bore us all to tears. I mean, she's like that with Freddie so she was bound to be ten times worse with a brand-new baby.

But the strange thing is, she wasn't. I mean, she isn't. She doesn't seem to care that much about the new baby after all now he's arrived, even though she'd wanted one so badly.

And I so wanted Angie to meet him; tiny, fragile Henry, with his stick-like arms and legs and tiny waving fists and his wrinkled, red, furious little face.

I can't believe she still hasn't been around to see him. Angie's bonkers about babies.

But she's not speaking to me.

Not properly anyway. I mean, she does talk, she says 'Hi' in the morning and she'll answer a direct question like what did she watch on telly last night, but in as few words as possible. She doesn't seek me out, in fact she avoids me as much as she can. She won't reply to my texts so I don't bother any more.

It's obvious she believed poisonous Gemma that I'd been with Si at her party. The Gemstones are always sucking up to her, delighted that they've succeeded in breaking us up.

But the worst thing is, I've seen Si hanging around her once or twice. I wonder what he's been telling her?

Don't go out with him again, Ange, he's not worth it.

One day I bump into her, literally, as I walk into our form room at the end of the day just as she's coming out.

'Sorry!' she says automatically and stands back against the door to let me pass, her eyes downcast. There's no one else in the classroom. I stop in front of her.

'I didn't do it you know,' I say.

'What?' She raises her eyes to meet mine.

'I didn't go with Si at the party. I wouldn't do that.' I hold her gaze levelly.

'I know.'

'What did you say?'

Her face softens. 'I know you wouldn't.'

My body floods with relief. 'It was Gemma,' I hear myself saying. 'She went off with him.'

Angie frowns. 'Why didn't you tell me at the time?'

'Because I knew you liked him! I didn't want to upset you, spoil your Christmas. I'm sorry, Ange.'

She shrugs. 'I don't care about him any more.'

'Good!' I say, my tongue running away with me. 'Because he might be gorgeous-looking and . . . and dead sexy . . . and a great dancer . . . but he's a creep, Ange. He'll try it on with anyone!'

Angie stares at me thoughtfully.

'Did he try it on with you Gabby?'

I can feel my face getting warm.

'I danced with him at the party,' I confess. 'That's all. Nothing happened.'

'Did you kiss him that night?'

'No.'

She studies me carefully. 'According to the Gemstones, he's told everyone he's snogged you.'

I can feel the warm blood flooding my cheeks and I shake my head vehemently. 'No, it wasn't like that, it wasn't that night . . .'

Angie's eyes open wide in surprise.

'When the hell was it then?'

'Look, Angie,' I say desperately, 'we have to talk. I need to explain . . .'

She doesn't give me a chance. She stalks off, her face blank with shock.

And now she won't talk to me at all.

Well done, Gabby. You really handled that one well.

Not.

When I get home that day from school, Gran is there! She's flying round the house with her broomstick (well, the hoover, actually), her face set grim.

'Where's Mum?' I yell above the noise. She switches it off and scowls at me.

'Gone to pick the boys up from school. She's left *him* upstairs.' She jerks her head towards the bedroom from where I can hear thin wails now the hoover's stopped whining. Why doesn't anyone call Henry by his name?

'She should've taken him with her. He's hungry if you ask me.' Gran sniffs her disapproval.

'He's always hungry. Are you feeling better, Gran?'

'Not really. But there's no point in lying in bed feeling sorry for yourself, is there?' Gran's face is a mask of righteousness. I get the feeling she's not talking about herself, it's Mum she's having a go at. In the past I've often conspired with my down-to-earth grandmother against my giddy mother, sharing a secret joke together about her. 'Not like some people,' she prompts, confirming my suspicions.

Suddenly I don't want to be part of this.

'I'll go and get him, shall I?' I ask and whip upstairs, not waiting for an answer. My parents' bedroom is in darkness and it smells rank. In the corner of the room, Henry is wailing in his cot. I bend over to study him.

'You're not even crying properly,' I say sternly. 'You've got no tears.'

He stops crying, distracted by my voice, and his eyes, which I know are not yet capable of creating real tears, strive to focus on me.

'You stink too,' I say conversationally. He's still, as if he's listening carefully.

'Smelly bum!' I remark and he watches me, concentrating hard.

'Gemma's a smelly bum too,' I say, 'and Jade, and Pearl and Ruby. They're all smelly bums.'

His mouth twitches as if he wants to laugh and I stroke his cheek gently with my finger. It quivers in a tiny spasm of pleasure.

'Angie's not a smelly bum though,' I say regretfully. 'Angie's nice.'

His face crumples as if he's about to cry. Can he really understand what I'm saying? I reach down for him before he starts yelling again. He's so tiny, he could break if I'm not careful. Gently, I place one hand under his back, feeling his sharp little shoulder blades jutting through his skin like keys in a soft leather purse. I put the other one under his bottom and lift him up out of the cot on to my shoulder. 'Let's get you cleaned up then, shall we?'

His tiny fingers flutter against my hair. Despite the pungent pong of dirty nappy it feels good. I hold him upright, my hand cradling his head. You've got to do that to tiny babies, support their heads.

'He knows you.'

I turn. Gran is at the door watching us.

'You're good with him. You calm him down.'

'Do I?'

She nods and reaches out for him. 'Give him to me, he needs changing. You go down and make us both a nice cup of tea.'

'No,' I say, turning away from her and pressing him closer to me, possessively. 'It's all right. You make the tea and I'll change him. I'm used to it now.'

Mum doesn't come home for ages. Dad's home before her. He looks happy for once.

'Where are the boys?' he asks, looking round the unusually clean and quiet house. 'Where's your mother?' There's something different about him, like he's got something exciting he can't wait to tell us about. Probably the footsie's gone back up. Big deal.

'Haven't a clue,' I say grimly. I'm fed up to the back teeth. I've been walking up and down with Henry for so long, patting his bum, trying to coax him off to sleep, my arms are aching. How can such a little squirt feel so heavy? I suppose it's like carrying a bag of potatoes round with you for a couple of hours. 'She went to get the boys from school. He needs a feed but I don't know where she's got to.'

'He hasn't been fed since lunchtime!' Gran puts her oar in. She's doubly cross because she's cooked us all a lovely supper, roast chicken and all the trimmings, but it's all dried up now in the oven. I tried to eat mine but Henry howled with fury when I put him down so I had to give up.

'Haven't we got any formula milk?' asks Dad.

229

'Mum won't let him have it. She wants to feed him herself.'

'Then she should be here with him! Here, pass him over.' I put Henry into his arms and he immediately starts squawking. (Henry, I mean, not Dad.) I can't help feeling smug.

I think Gran's right. He knows me. He's definitely not so sure about Dad because he rapidly builds up into a screech fest, his mouth wide open, as plaintive and insistent as a baby bird.

'He's starving,' says Gran.

'Where the hell is she?' says Dad, rocking Henry so hard his head wobbles dangerously. (Again, I mean Henry, not Dad. No, actually, his head lurches about a bit too.)

'Dad! You've got to support him!'

'Here!' he says, thrusting Henry back at me. 'You take him! I'm going out to get some formula!' He slams the door behind him.

Wouldn't you know it? He hasn't been gone five minutes and there's a key in the door and the sound of chatter and Mum and the boys are back, their faces alight. Freddie is carrying a helium-filled balloon and has smears of ketchup on his face and school sweatshirt. 'We've been out for tea,' he announces unnecessarily, shining with pleasure.

'We've brought some home for you!' Felix holds a brown paper carrier bag aloft.

Gran clicks her tongue reprovingly. 'It's your baby that needs feeding, Pauline, not us.'

The light dies from Mum's face and unconsciously her hand moves to her breast. She looks at Henry guiltily as he lets out a pathetic mewl, and then at the clock.

'Oh dear,' she says contritely. 'Is it that time already?'

'He's had nothing since lunchtime!' says Gran doggedly. Mum looks as if she's going to cry.

'Here you are, Mum. Feed him now.' I pass him to her and she sits down heavily on the sofa with him in her arms. Henry, sensing perhaps that sustenance is on its way at last, screams frantically.

'I just wanted to give them a treat,' she says, looking up at us. Tears well up in her eyes. 'I forgot him for once. Just for once. I forgot all about him.'

I glance in alarm at Gran. Her mouth is tight with disapproval.

'That's all right, you didn't mean to,' I say, sitting down by her side and putting my arm around her. 'Don't blame yourself.'

She shakes her head like a child. 'No, you don't get it. You don't get it at all. None of you do.' Tears roll down her cheeks as Henry wails miserably in her arms.

'Get a grip, Pauline!' Gran says angrily. 'You've got a baby to look after!'

'I *wanted* to forget him,' she whispers.

'Feed him, Mum,' I plead. 'Feed him then he'll stop crying.'

'I can't.' She sobs out loud. 'He doesn't want me.'

'Pauline, stop this!' Gran's tone is cross but her face looks frightened. Freddie puts his thumb in his mouth then takes it out and starts to cry. Felix stares fixedly at Mum, biting his lower lip. The front door opens.

'I've got the milk,' shouts Dad. 'I hope it's the right stuff. I told the woman he was prem.'

He stops dead when he sees us all. 'Where the hell have you been?' he asks Mum and then notices she's crying. He pauses in front of us uncertainly. 'What's going on?'

'Shall I give him a bottle, Mum?' I ask.

She says nothing, her head bent. Henry's cries become more desperate.

'Pauline,' says Gran urgently, 'I know you don't want to bottle feed but just this once won't hurt. You're tired out and the poor little man, he's famished . . .'

Mum's shoulders heave, silently.

'Please, Mum,' I beg, 'let me . . .'

Suddenly she pushes him into my arms, so savagely I have to grab him before he falls to the floor.

'Here! Take him!' she sobs. 'Do what you want with him. He hates me anyway. I don't care any more.'

Before we have time to do or say anything to stop her, she runs straight out of the front door as Henry, in shock, stops crying at last.

She came home late that night. The house was quiet. Felix and Freddie had gone to bed and Henry was still, unbelievably, asleep, even though Mum had been gone for ages. It was the longest he'd ever slept in one go. Gran had gone home on the bus hours before. She'd wanted to stay till Mum got home but Dad, appearing remarkably calm in the circumstances, said, 'No need, she'll come home when she's ready.'

But he's getting more anxious as the time goes by, I can tell, because he keeps looking at the clock. Eventually, he tries her mobile, but it goes off upstairs so he fetches it and scrawls through the address book. There are hardly any numbers in it, just his and mine and people like the doctor and dentist.

'Who's her best friend, Gabby?' he asks.

'I dunno.' I think for a minute. 'She hasn't really got one, has she? She used to know people from yoga but she hasn't been for ages.'

'Where could she have got to?' He stands up and pulls the curtain aside and peers out into the darkness. Suddenly I'm scared.

'Do you think we should tell someone, Dad?'

He turns around and looks at me, considering. He knows what I mean. Should we tell the police? A sigh escapes him and he grabs his keys from the coffee table.

'I'll just drive around for a minute first, have a look for her.' I suddenly realize Dad hasn't had a drink tonight, for the first time since I can remember. 'Won't be long,' he says and, unusually, bends down to plant a kiss on my head. 'Leave you in charge, hey?'

I nod, not trusting myself to speak. But then there's the sound of the key in the front door and it swings open and Mum walks in.

'Mum!' I yell, rushing towards her. 'Where have you been?'

'Just out,' she says and turns away from me, her arms hugged tight to her chest. I stop, as stunned as if she'd slapped me in the face. I'd never thought about it before but in all my days I can never remember my mother not welcoming me with open arms, quite literally. It was what she did, my mother: she hugged and cuddled and clutched and clung on to you until often you felt suffocated by her love.

And she never once turned away.

'I'm going to bed,' she says. She looks exhausted. Her hair has escaped from its top-knot and is trailing untidily down on to her shoulders and she has dark circles under her eyes. She climbs the stairs slowly, head down, arms still folded protectively in front of her body. She hasn't looked at us once.

'Good idea,' says Dad, staring up at her. From their bedroom a thin wail is heard. Mum freezes. 'Don't worry,' he says gently, 'I'll see to him. You get some rest.'

She turns around and looks at us for the first time. Her eyes are blank and her face is devoid of expression and colour. She's like a brittle plastic bottle that someone has tipped upside down and drained the contents out of, leaving just the empty casing. She nods blindly and continues up to their room and Dad follows behind as if he wants to catch her if she falls. In a few minutes he's back downstairs again, baby in his arms.

'Shall I hold him while you make up a bottle?' I ask.

'No, it's all right,' he says. 'You get to bed. We'll manage, won't we, Henry?' He looks down at the baby and rocks him gently. 'Your mum's done in, mate,' he says quietly. 'Looks like you'll have to put up with your old dad for a bit.'

'Night, Dad.'

At the top of the stairs I glance down. I can see,

through the open door of the lounge, Dad, sprawling in the armchair, with tiny Henry snuggled on to his chest. One hand taps his padded little bum while the other pats his back in a gentle rhythm that matches the beat of the song he's singing softly to his baby son. I recognize the tune. It's a Beatles' number. He used to sing it to Freddie.

He used to sing it to me.

I don't know what's wrong with Mum but now I'm not quite so scared any more.

At first school is horrible without Angie. She avoids me. It's not so bad during lessons, but breaktimes and lunchtimes I really miss her. Kelvin's started a juggling club and she goes along there most lunchtimes. Loads of the Year 9 girls have joined. She doesn't ask me to go with her. I wouldn't anyway because the Gemstones have signed up for it. They want to learn how to twirl batons so they can start a cheerleading group. Vomit. I'm sure they're getting mixed up with majorettes.

One day, I'm sitting in the canteen on my own, eating a sandwich and feeling like a real saddo, when a voice says, 'Mind if I join you?' It's Si. I glance around. A few tables away, Jade nudges Gemma in the ribs. I feel anger rising inside me but I shrug as if I'm not bothered.

'It's a free country.'

He treats me to his full-on smile but it's lost its appeal.

He sits down opposite and offers me a chip. I shake my head and crush up the remains of my sandwich, not hungry any more.

'I'm finished,' I say and get up to go. His hand comes out to grasp my wrist.

'Fancy going out tonight, Gabby?' he asks.

I can't believe my ears.

'Yeah?' he prompts.

'Get lost,' I say.

'Go on,' he says. 'You know you want to really.'

He is so conceited! I want to punch his grinning face.

'You don't get it, do you?' I snap. 'Angie and I were best mates!'

I can feel everyone's eyes on us, but I don't care.

He smiles lazily. '*Were*. That's the point. You're not any more. There's nothing to stop you now. I'm all yours.'

I snatch my hand away. 'I wouldn't go out with you if you were the last person on earth!'

As I stalk off a cheer goes up in the canteen. Behind me I hear Si saying, 'She loves me really!' and everyone laughs.

Ignorant, arrogant pig!

Fed up with being on my own, I start bringing my tennis racket to school and cadging a game with whoever's playing at lunchtime. It's usually the Year 10s and 11s who grab the courts but they let me join in if they're short of a player because I'm pretty good. Before long they automatically count me in (they should too, I'm better than most of them!) and soon I'm playing every day. At least I'm keeping my hand in now Dad's stopped paying out for lessons at the club.

Actually, I find I quite like hanging out with the upper school, they're so much more mature than my year. Well, some of them are: I guess Si wasn't exactly Mr Maturity, was he? Maybe it's just the ones who play tennis; I mean, if you're intent on playing a game, you can't be hanging around gossiping and giggling and flirting all the time, which is just as well because I'm off men.

After a while, I find myself a partner. It's Tug, of all people. He's pretty good considering he's only just started playing and he's never had a lesson in his life. He's got a mean backhand and he's all too pleased to pick up tips from me.

He's all right, Tug. I reckon he's only started playing tennis so he can get away from Si.

Life's not too bad in some ways.

I miss Angie though.

At home everything settles down, sort of. Dad makes an effort and drops the boys off at school for a day or two so that Mum can sleep in, because it's pretty obvious she's knackered. But then Mum gets anxious about him being late for work and insists that he goes back to his normal working day, even though he says it's OK. When Gran offers to come round and give Mum a hand she won't hear of it.

'Why is everyone making such a fuss?' she snaps. 'Honestly, I'm not incapable you know. I have brought up three children already! It's no big deal! Just because you only had one . . .' Her voice tails away and Gran goes home looking hurt.

It's not like Mum to be irritable. She's changed since the baby was born. It's funny, I thought she'd have been over the moon – after all, she'd got what she wanted, a brand-new baby – but ever since Henry was born, she's been . . . different. She's permanently tired but she reckons she can't sleep, even though baby Hen is sleeping loads more now, since he's started having bottles. He looks better too, more like a ripe grapefruit nowadays than a wizened apple. She still feeds him herself as well but not so much now, I think her milk is drying up. Sometimes she seems to forget about him altogether. I've come home more than once to find him screaming his head off upstairs and her in the lounge watching television with the door shut and the volume turned right up.

She's crabby with Dad too which is a real turnabout

because she was always the one who was trying to appease him. I feel a bit sorry for him nowadays; he looks bemused as if he doesn't know quite what to do for the best. She's got no patience with me or the boys either. I never thought I'd feel sorry for Freddie but I did the day she chucked his dinner in the bin.

The weather had been scorching. When I get home from school that day, I'm baking hot and dog-tired. The air is heavy and sultry and I've just played a singles match with Tug and had to work really hard to beat him. I think I'd better stop giving him tips, he's getting too good. Everyone's at home, even Dad who seems to be leaving the office earlier and earlier nowadays. I can hardly blame him; it must be unbearable in Central London in this weather.

He's in the back garden playing cricket with the boys. Baby Hen is lying quietly on his back in his pram in the shade of the sycamore tree, mesmerized by the ever-changing pattern of light and leaves overhead. Mum's in the kitchen getting supper ready. It's like a picture from *Homes and Gardens*. The article would be headed up, 'A sanctum of summertime serenity'.

I flop down on my back on the grass gratefully, offering myself up like a sacrifice to the early-evening sun. Overhead, I notice storm clouds are gathering. The heat, even at this late hour, is intense and I feel myself becoming drowsy. As if from an increasing distance I can hear the distinctive rasp of magpies in the trees; the clunk of ball on bat; Dad's deep voice issuing advice to Felix who's in batting position; Freddie's high, excitable chatter; and through the open patio doors, the clatter of cutlery and crockery as Mum lays the table for supper. Soon the sounds recede and I drift off to sleep.

Of course, the peaceful, Sheraton–Hogg family scene couldn't possibly last for long. Even before the first drops of rain fall, Freddie wakes me up with his constant whining that it's his turn to bat. He uses his usual effective tactic of repeating the same demand over and over again. 'It's my turn, it's my turn, it's my turn,' he reiterates till at last Dad gives in and allows the grateful Felix to relinquish his Hannibal Lecter helmet to his whingeing little brother.

At the same time Mum calls, 'Supper's ready!' and Freddie howls, 'Noooo!' and hurls the helmet to the ground in frustration. Dad shouts at him and hauls him by his collar into the house. Henry, already startled by Freddie's noisy protest, starts squawking in earnest as the rain splatters through the tree on to his pram.

Inside the house it's obvious Mum's made an effort. She's laid the table in the dining room with a cloth and flowers from the garden and the old glasses that have been passed down through the generations in Dad's family that are, apparently, worth a bomb. There's a bottle of wine for her and Dad and in the middle of the table she's placed the cut-glass decanter, part of the same set, filled with lemonade for us. Just like old times, the whole family assembled. Bar one.

'Shall I fetch Henry in?' I ask helpfully. 'It's starting to rain.'

'No!' she says sharply. 'Let's try and have one meal in peace. Sit at the table, we're ready to eat.'

Pardon me for asking! I sit down grumpily.

'What's the occasion?' asks Dad jovially, perking up at the sight of the wine.

Mum clucks her tongue tetchily as she moves between the kitchen and the dining room, bearing bowls of steaming food. 'Does there have to be an occasion? Can't we just sit down together to a civilized meal?'

'Of course we can!' says Dad heartily, reaching for the wine-opener. 'Freddie! Stop snivelling!'

'Is it steak and kidney pie?' I groan as I spot gravy bubbling through a pastry topping. 'It's too hot for that!'

'I hate steak and kidney pie!' yells Freddie and bursts into fresh wails. Dad pulls the cork out and pours himself a glass of wine. Mum puts a bowl of green beans down next to it.

'I hate green beans!' roars Freddie and pushes the bowl away. It knocks Dad's glass of wine over. A huge red stain floods the white tablecloth and the wine drips down on to the carpet. Dad springs up and Freddie cowers into his chair but Dad just glares at him and grabs a cloth to mop up the wine. Outside, Henry, sensing he's been abandoned in what's rapidly turning into a rainstorm, turns up the volume and roars his disapproval.

'Shall I get the baby?' Felix rises from his seat. 'It's pouring down out there.'

'NO, I SAID!' yells Mum. 'SIT DOWN AND PASS ME YOUR PLATE!'

Dumbfounded, Felix sinks back down and does as he's told. Mum savagely doles out piles of food on to his plate. I hand it back to him and he looks at it glumly and passes it on to Dad who accepts it without a word.

'Not so much for me, Mum,' I say quietly.

'You'll eat what you're given!' she retorts and plonks a laden plate in front of me and then does the same for Felix.

'I don't want any,' hiccups Freddie woefully. Mum ignores him and loads his plate high with food. Her cheeks are red and her face is shiny with sweat. She slams the plate down in front of him then grabs hold of his chair and rams it tight into the table, so hard he nearly falls off. She picks up the knife and fork and pushes them into his hands.

'Eat!' she says, bending over him, her voice now menacingly quiet. He turns to look at her, his face tear-stained.

'Just eat it up, old chap,' says Dad encouragingly.

'I don't like it,' Freddie whispers.

'I spent all afternoon making that for you,' says Mum, through gritted teeth. 'Now eat it!'

Freddie shakes his head miserably.

'Eat it!' orders Mum and picks up a fork. She spears a potato and some meat and pastry and pushes it at Freddie's mouth. He resists, his lips clamped tightly together.

'EAT IT!' she screams, making us all jump. He sobs and his mouth opens and she forces it between his teeth. Bits of gravy-soaked meat and potato fall on to the table and Freddie makes a choking sound.

'Posy!' yells Dad and springs to his feet. 'What the hell do you think you're doing?'

Mum stands upright. She's shaking. Suddenly she drops Freddie's fork on to his plate with a clatter making us all jump. He bursts into tears.

'I can't do anything right, can I?' she screams. 'I can't feed the baby. I can't feed you!' She snatches up Freddie's plate and fork again and scoops the food into the bin. Then she grabs mine and does the same. When she seizes Dad's she doesn't even bother cleaning it off, she just chucks the whole thing, plate and contents, in the bin.

Then she picks up the decanter of lemonade and hurls it at the wall.

As the family heirloom smashes into hundreds of tiny fragments my mother sinks down on to the floor with her head in her hands and rocks backwards and forwards, howling so loudly it finally drowns out Freddie's sobbing and the cries of baby Hen, alone outside in the rain.

The three of us, Felix, Freddie and I, watch, transfixed in horror, as Dad kneels down in front of her. Gently, he takes her in his arms and rocks with her, to and fro, back and forth, making soft, soothing noises. 'There, there,' he croons. 'Ssh. It's all right. Shush now.'

He repeats the words again and again, patting her back at the same time, in the same gentle rhythm he used to settle his baby son just a few nights previously. Gradually her cries subside and her arms come up to cling round his neck. She calms down.

Outside the rain stops.

The storm is over.

The next day Dad stays home from work. Me, I'm glad to go to school, just to get away from the house, and I think the boys feel the same. Freddie is unbelievably co-operative: he actually manages to wash and dress himself, as if he feels he's got to be good or Mum will freak out again. Poor little kid, it wasn't his fault, it's Mum: she's all wired up at the moment.

I so want to talk to Angie about Mum but she doesn't give me the chance, she just says hello and turns away looking sad. This is rubbish, I don't know how we got to this state, but I know one thing, she's as miserable about it as I am. It's like my life has turned into a war zone. If Mum's a cluster bomb about to explode all over the place, then the Gemstones have lobbed a hand grenade at Angie and me, and we're so confused by all the smoke, we can't find a way to defuse it.

I'm not daft: I'm old enough to understand my

mother's having some sort of breakdown. I'm young enough to be scared witless about it. It's obvious things have got on top of Mum and she can't cope. If only I could just talk to Angie. Maybe her mum went funny when she had Talitha and Bolton. I remember Bolton being born though. I don't think she did.

One good thing. The health visitor turns up again. I don't know whether Dad called her or she wasn't fooled by the Super Mum routine after all, but anyway, she sees Mum and the baby and then Dad catches her on the way out and they have a bit of a chat.

So now we've got her keeping an eye on things and Gran back on her feet, and Dad around a bit more.

Between us all, Mum should be fine, shouldn't she?

At last it's the weekend and we all go out, everyone except Mum that is. Dad takes us to a theme park on Saturday and a stately home on Sunday. Even Henry comes in his pram with a supply of bottles. I recognize what Dad's doing so I go along with it. He's making sure Mum gets some rest.

'Your mother needs to catch up on her sleep,' explains Dad to me when he outlines his plans for the weekend. 'It's taken it out of her, having a baby . . .' His voice peters out.

I complete the sentence for him. '. . . at her age.'

He gives a huge sigh, then rallies again. 'So we'll all go

off and have some fun together and keep out of her hair for a while, hey, Gabby?'

Yeah, Dad. Like the idea of spending the weekend in the company of a balding middle-aged father, two mixed-up kids and a bawling, angry baby is my idea of a good time.

Still, someone has to look after poor Hen. None of this is his fault.

Freddie thinks it's an excellent idea. Mum has frightened the life out of him with her force-feeding act. I can't help but notice he's eaten everything up without complaint ever since. Maybe she should have let rip years ago. I'm only joking, it was really scary.

'Will Mum be all right without us?' asks Felix looking worried.

'She'll be fine,' says Dad and ruffles his hair. Felix looks up and gives him a small, relieved smile. Dad's so much nicer to Felix lately. He hasn't gone on about boarding school for a while.

In fact, Dad's so much nicer full stop.

Why do they have to take it in turns to be nice, my mother and father? Why can't they both be nice at the same time?

Anyway, as it turns out, we have a brilliant time. We've been to the theme park before. It's got loads of boring exhibitions but for once Dad doesn't insist we trail around looking at them all. Instead we spend all our time on the rides, throwing ourselves down giant slides, shooting the rapids in wooden barrels and hurtling through the air at breathtaking speed on the brand-new, death-defying rollercoaster. It's heart-pounding, mind-blowing, thrill-seeking stuff.

Dad sits with the pram watching us. I can tell he's made up to see how much Felix is enjoying the adrenalin rush. Last time we came here a few years ago, Felix was really wussy and had to be rescued from the demon drop. This time he loves it. I reckon it's because he hasn't got Dad breathing down his neck all the time urging him on to try things he's not ready for. He can decide for himself because Dad's got his hands full with the baby. Today Felix plummets down the fifty-metre shaft and climbs back up for more while Dad looks on proudly. Afterwards he rewards us with big sticks of candy floss.

I'm not being nasty but sometimes it's OK after all to have just one parent around. You get more treats that way.

The next day we go along to this stately home Dad wants us to see. Apparently he went there when he was a kid. If Dad's interested in anything at all outside of the stock market and his wine cellar, it's history and old houses. Well, I never said my dad was a bundle of laughs, did I? I'm expecting this to be totally tedious and I'm not wrong. We shuffle from room to room looking at faded tapestries and upholstered chairs, four-poster beds and chests of drawers, and oil paintings of men in wigs staring out glumly from their framed prisons. Mega-boring. There are huge signs everywhere saying 'DO NOT TOUCH' and most of it is chained off from the general public as if they're afraid we're going to stick a fusty old footstool or a chipped chamberpot under our coats and leg it as fast as we can.

'It's all minging,' I grumble to Felix but I might as well have saved my breath. He's standing in front of two bewigged plaster figures dressed in the costume of the day. The man is wearing knee-length breeches, stockings and shoes with buckles, a shirt, a waistcoat and a frock coat.

'He looks like Dad in his three-piece suit!' I giggle and dig him in the ribs, but he's turned his attention to the woman. She's wearing a long dress with a bodice and a full skirt, made from silk I think, gathered up at the bottom to reveal an underskirt and a wooden frame.

'Imagine having to cart all that around with you everywhere you went,' breathes Felix, his face alive with interest.

'Look at her face,' I say. On her cheeks and forehead,

tiny black stars and crescent moons are painted. 'That is so cool.'

'Sometimes they did that to cover up pockmarks,' Felix explains. He is so clever, he knows everything. A man stops to listen. 'There are more costumes in here,' says Freddie. We enter another room where they're displayed on metal frames.

'These must have been what the servants wore,' he says, examining them carefully.

'How can you tell?'

'They're very plain. See the collar on that dress? If it belonged to a rich woman it would have been fancier, made of lace probably, like the one out there.'

'Very perceptive,' says a voice. 'It's actually made of linen.' It's the same man. He's about Dad's age with a shock of white hair and he's wearing a badge that says he's a guide.

Felix turns to him with interest. 'People must have been much shorter then. That dress is tiny. It wouldn't even fit my sister.'

'Maybe. But a maid would be very young in those days, not much older than you, young man.'

I think about it, imagining what it must have been like to work for a living at the age of ten. Waiting hand and foot on posh people; cleaning up after them; chucking out their ashes from the fire; emptying their chamberpots! I shudder. No wonder Gran is always going on about how we should help more around the house. I expect it was like that in her day.

Felix studies the dress with interest. 'Actually, I think it might not be a full-length dress anyway. If you look at the dimensions, the skirt doesn't look long enough.'

'That's quite right.' The guide looks at him admiringly. 'The skirts would have been worn a bit shorter then so they didn't trail in the mud. In the seventeenth century the servants would be more concerned about keeping their dresses clean than showing a bit of ankle. This wasn't the Victorian period you know.'

Felix nods knowledgeably. 'So that's why they wore dark colours.'

How come he notices all this stuff? The guide is practically wetting himself with delight. Felix must be such a find.

'Absolutely. They would have owned two outfits each, one to wear and one to wash.'

'And the men?'

'The same. Knee-length breeches, a linen shirt and a waistcoat. All very plain. It was the rich people who wore the fancy outfits.'

'The designer stuff,' says Felix.

'Exactly,' says the man and grins at him in satisfaction.

'All right, you two?' asks Dad, coming up behind with

Freddie and Henry who today is clamped to his chest in a sling. 'Not being a nuisance, are they?' he adds, like we're about six.

'Goodness me, no!' says the guide emphatically, then suddenly he stops. 'Leonard?' he asks. 'Leonard Hogg?'

Dad looks startled then he smiles and thrusts his hand at the guide. 'Hugo Hall! Well I never!' They do that shaking hands, clapping shoulders man-thing for a while, chuckling loudly all the time as if it was the funniest thing ever that they'd come across each other in a manky old mansion in the middle of nowhere. Which possibly it is when you consider that the guy sounds as if he was named after a listed building himself.

'I shouldn't be surprised to find you here,' says Dad at last, letting poor Hugo's hand go before it's irreversibly dislocated. He turns to us. 'Hugo was chairman of the historical society at school,' he says in revered tones as if he's announcing he'd won double gold in the Olympic Games.

'And your grandfather was the secretary!' announces Hugo.

'Father,' corrects Felix. 'He's our father.'

'Good grief,' blurts Hugo, eyeing Henry in his sling doubtfully. 'You've been busy, old man.'

I like Hugo. There's something of Felix in him. He says what he thinks.

Dad smiles ruefully. 'Late starter, I'm afraid.'

Hugo rallies. 'You've got a clever lad here, I must say. Reminds me very much of you at that age.'

'Really?' Dad looks surprised.

'Bright spark, you can tell. Enquiring mind. He'll go far.'

Dad puts his arm round Felix's shoulders and smiles proudly.

'Like you,' continues Hugo. 'What did you end up as? President of the British Museum? Curator of the Victoria and Albert?'

'No, actually I just went into the City.' Dad looks a bit crestfallen.

'Ah well,' says Hugo, 'never mind.' He sounds disappointed. 'I had to make a living myself, you know. Still, now I'm retired I'm indulging myself with this little job. Should have done it years ago.'

He bends down and speaks confidingly in Felix's ear. 'You make sure you don't waste your talents, my boy. Do what *you* want to do, not what someone else tells you to.' He straightens up and looks Dad straight in the eye. 'Bright spark,' he reiterates. 'A real chip off the old block.'

So it turns out the day at the stately home wasn't so bad after all. Dad treats us all to a cream tea, then we stop for burgers on the way home so Mum won't have to bother to cook. I could get used to this. I must say, Dad seems far more generous lately than he's been for ages. He's certainly not angsting so much nowadays about how much everything costs.

Maybe he's won the lottery.

I decide once and for all that if Angie and I are ever going to be mates again, then it's up to me to put things right. After all, it was my fault for kissing Si back, even though at the time I couldn't help myself. It's weird, he gives me the creeps now; I can't understand what I ever saw in him. I hate the way he preys on girls, collecting snogs (and more, according to the gossip!) like scalps on a belt. Pervert. He and Gemma would make a good couple, they should just forget about everyone else and get on with it.

So this morning, I don't look away when Angie walks into the classroom. I wait till she goes to her locker which is next to mine and then I walk over and insert my key in my lock and say, 'Hi.'

'Hi,' she replies without looking up. I take a deep breath and add, 'How you doing?'

'Fine.'

'How's the juggling?'

'Good.' She turns away.

Desperately, I put my hand out to stop her. 'Angie?'

'What?' She won't look me in the eye. Instead she studies my hand on her arm in a distasteful, almost puzzled way as if it's an abnormal growth that has suddenly manifested itself.

'Come and see the baby. Come and see him, please!'

She's still as a statue. I start pleading.

'Please, Ange. He's growing so fast you wouldn't believe it.'

'What's he like?'

I knew she wouldn't be able to resist it, she's mad about babies. I think of Henry with his funny little alien face and try to think how I could possibly describe him so that Angie would just have to come and see him. Difficult. Then I remember the baby on the front of the Mothercare catalogue, the cute one with the towel on his head.

'I'm not kidding, he's gorgeous. He's got blond hair and big blue eyes and rosy cheeks. You'll love him to bits.'

A little frown appears between her eyebrows.

'Is he smiling yet?'

'All the time! He laughs out loud!'

'Really?' She looks surprised by this piece of information. 'Has he got any teeth yet?'

'Loads!' She looks very surprised this time so I backtrack quickly. 'Well, some. Two at the bottom and two at the top. Little white ones . . .'

She nods sagely. 'I suppose he's sitting up by now?'

'Nearly!' Gosh, is he supposed to be doing that already? An image springs into my mind of tiny Henry lying inert in his cot, as soft and squashy as a bean bag, but I repress it firmly. A memory dashes in to fill its space of Angie in raptures when Bolton learned to crawl. 'Mum thinks he'll be crawling soon.'

This has been the longest conversation we've had for weeks. I offer up a prayer that it'll work, that she'll want to be friends with me again now I've got this prize-winning, high-achieving, designer-collection baby brother. But it doesn't seem to have worked. She's gone quiet on me. My heart sinks.

Then a funny thing happens. I feel her silently shaking beside me, then she starts making a peculiar noise as if she's choking.

'Are you all right?' I ask, wondering if I should offer to bang her on the back.

She clears her throat. 'You don't *do* babies, do you?'

'What?'

Her eyes meet mine, full of amusement. Is she laughing at me?

'Teeth? Sitting up? Crawling? How old is he?'

'Five weeks and four days.'

She sounds as if she's gasping for air.

'He's advanced for his age,' I add lamely.

This time she shrieks with laughter and several people look up. It's not that funny.

Angie seems to think so though because I haven't seen her laugh like this for ages. Not since we fell out. I sigh. Maybe it's time to be honest after all.

'OK. He's not advanced at all. He can't sit up or crawl and he hasn't got a tooth in his head. He's not gorgeous either. He's as bald as my dad and just as ugly. He's got a face like a turnip and I haven't got a clue what colour his eyes are because they're permanently screwed up tight while he bawls his head off.'

'They're blue.'

'Pardon?'

'His eyes are blue. All babies are born with blue eyes.'

'Are they?' I pause for a minute to digest this nugget of information. It must be right if Angie says so. 'Actually, I think I knew that already.'

Her eyes soften.

'I miss you.'

My heart floods with gladness.

'I miss you too.'

'Angelina and Gabrielle, how long do I have to wait for you to stop talking and sit down,' calls our form teacher. From the corner of my eye I see Jade nudging Gemma in the ribs.

Angie giggles. 'Just like old times.'

I nod, so thankful I could burst. 'See you lunchtime?' I ask, not daring to take anything for granted.

'You bet. Oh.' Her face is full of concern. 'I've got juggling!'

'That's OK,' I say, remembering. 'I've got tennis.'

We stare at each other in consternation. Suddenly it seems weird, us both doing separate activities.

'You can come and play tennis with me if you like,' I suggest.

Angie wrinkles her nose. 'Or I could show you how to juggle.'

'OK.'

Her face lights up.

'But not lunchtime, I've arranged to play with Tug.'

She grins meaningfully. 'Are you and Tug . . . you know?'

'No!' I stare at her in amazement. 'We just play tennis together.'

'Oh, right. Just wondered. Silly me.' She looks suitably apologetic.

'What about you and Si?' I ask, hesitantly. 'I saw you talking to him.'

'NO WAY!!!' she explodes. 'He kept asking me out for

a while but I told him where to go!'

'Me too!' I admit.

'I know, I was in the canteen. I heard it!'

We grin at each other happily.

'What a creep!' I say.

Angie nods in agreement. 'What was all that about, Gabby? We don't even fancy him any more.'

'I don't think I ever did.'

Suddenly Angie flings her arms around me. 'Sod him!' she says. 'Come and do some juggling at breaktime.'

'OK.' I'm brimming with happiness.

'GABRIELLE AND ANGELINA, SIT!'

'Sorry, miss,' we chorus and sink into our rightful places next to each other. Gemma turns round and scowls at us both. Angie and I exchange glances and giggle. I couldn't care less what Gemma thinks. She can't hurt me now. Angie and I are friends again.

That feeling lasts all morning: through two periods of French and maths which don't seem as boring as normal; during break when Angie teaches me the rudiments of juggling in ten minutes flat and I make the most amazing progress, even though I say so myself; on through double science which suddenly seems interesting for once; and all through lunchtime, when I gobble my usual tuna sandwich which today tastes delicious with Angie beside me for company, before playing a doubles match with

Tug against a couple of Year 11s in which we tear the opposition to shreds.

'Wow!' Tug says at the end. 'You played brilliantly!'

'I did, didn't I?' I don't care if he does thinks I'm big-headed. Today is special and I've decided that modesty is an overrated virtue!

He laughs. 'What's up with you today? You're different.'

I wave at Angie who's making her way towards us, now juggling has finished in the hall. 'Angie and I are mates again.'

'Good!' he says and grins. He looks genuinely pleased. 'I always thought you two were mad to let a creep like Si come between you.'

'I know. It was all a stupid misunderstanding. I never liked him anyway.' I've convinced myself of this now.

'Didn't you?' His voice sounds serious.

'Didn't you what?' asks Angie.

'Nothing!' Tug and I both say simultaneously, and we all laugh.

'Wonder what's so funny?' says a familiar, snidey voice. Gemma appears before us, a supercilious expression upon her pointed features, like she knows something we don't. Behind her Ruby, Pearl and Jade are lined up, smirking, a backing group to her solo performance. Despite myself, I feel a clutch of fear. What are they up to now?

'Get lost, Gemma,' says Angie coldly, 'and take your sad little cling-ons with you.'

Gemma ignores her and stares at me, her upper lip curled in a very unbecoming sneer. 'Just thought you'd like to hear the news, Gabby. Because we know how much you hate the way some people help themselves to things from shops without paying for them, don't we, girls?'

'Yes,' says Jade. 'You'd never do anything like that, would you, Gab-ri-eeeelle?' She lingers over my name, drawing it out from her mouth like a piece of chewing gum until it sounds twisted and disgusting.

'She told me all about your thieving ways,' says Angie dismissively. 'Sad creatures.'

'Not as sad as some people,' says Pearl, stung. 'At least *we* got away with it!' They all cackle as if she's said something hilarious. What are they on about?

Gemma studies me. She's loving this. Whatever her game is, she's going to draw every possible drop of perverted pleasure from it.

'Only we've just been down to the precinct,' she continues as if she hasn't been interrupted.

'Been at it again?' remarks Angie sarkily but Gemma smiles smugly, as if she's paid her a compliment.

Tug tuts. 'Naughty, naughty!' he taunts, shaking his head in mock disapproval at the Gemstones. 'You know you're not supposed to be out of school at lunchtime, girls. Whatever will you do next? Forget your homework?'

I dart him a quick look of gratitude. He winks at me. Much better tactics. He's made them look stupid and childish by laughing at them. Gemma's face hardens.

'Well if we hadn't gone, we'd have missed the fun, wouldn't we, girls?' She looks at them to tug their strings and they all snigger obediently like the puppets they are. They're getting on my nerves. Not one of them is capable of acting alone, not even Gemma. I wonder how any one of them would have coped with what I've had to put up with for the past few weeks?

Suddenly I realize they don't scare me any more.

'What fun?' I say.

'Forget it, Gabby,' says Angie. 'They're not worth it.'

But I can't forget it. I'm fed up with Gemma interfering in my life. I'm mad at the way I've allowed her to split Angie and me up for so long. How dare she?

Some people say you see red when you're angry. I'm starting to see orange, purple, black and blue as well.

'Come on then, Big Gob!' I challenge her. 'Tell us the news.'

Gemma looks momentarily surprised at the insult, then her mouth twists into a cruel, mirthless smile.

'Leave it, Gabs,' warns Angie urgently, slipping her arm

through mine. 'Don't bother with them.'

I shrug her away and take a step forward. 'Tell me!' I repeat, thrusting my face close up to Gemma's. 'Tell me!'

Involuntarily she takes a pace back and stumbles and the Gemstones stand back out of her way, breaking up the line of defence. I glare at them all, blazing with fury.

'LOSERS!' I dismiss them all, derisively. 'You know nothing! You're just stirring as usual. Now, get lost the lot of you and leave me alone!'

'Losers, yeah? We know nothing, yeah?' Gemma splutters, knowing she's lost face, her voice high and blustering like the wind on a hot day, her eyes wild. 'Well that's where you're wrong, see? We're not the losers, you are!'

'Yeah, yeah!' My voice, in contrast, is low with contempt. I should've done this years ago. 'How do you make that one out then?'

'Because,' Gemma pauses for effect, seasoned performer as she is, regaining control, 'we've just seen your snooty mother being taken away in a police car. She's been arrested for shop-lifting, Posh Girl. So who's the loser now?'

266

Game, set and match to Gemma. I didn't see that one coming, not by a long shot. You know that bit at the end of every Wimbledon Final when the victor falls to his or her knees in triumph? Well, in this case, I was the loser who fell down in shame only luckily I was propped up on one side by Angie and the other by Tug, both of whom grab an arm and keep me upright. Which is maybe just as well, because if I'd been capable of standing alone on my own two feet I think I would have slapped Gemma's stupid gloating grin off her stupid gleeful face.

In fact, Tug is doubly useful because he tells the Gemstones to clear off in very precise Anglo-Saxon terms that leave them in no doubt whatsoever that they're not wanted round here any more.

So they do.

'Don't listen to her,' says Angie, as they fade away. 'You know what a liar she is.' But her face is dismayed because we both know Gemma couldn't have made this one up, she hasn't got the imagination. And I've seen the way Mum's been acting lately – she's capable of anything.

The bell goes for afternoon school.

'What am I going to do?' I ask, bewildered.

'Phone your dad,' suggests Tug who seems to have his wits about him. I pull out my phone and scroll through for Dad's work number, which luckily I've added since Henry's arrival when I learnt my lesson about keeping useful contact phone numbers close to hand.

At last a bored-sounding female voice answers. 'Babcock and Burton? How can I help you?'

'I need to speak to my father,' I explain. 'Leonard Sheraton–Hogg. It's an emergency.'

There's silence at the end of the line. 'Hello? Hello?' I prompt. 'Are you still there? Can you hear me?'

The receptionist clears her throat. 'Yes, madam, I can hear you. I'm afraid I'm unable to put you through though to Mr Hogg.'

'Why not?' The line goes quiet again. 'Look,' I explain desperately, 'you don't seem to understand. I need to get hold of him urgently.'

She gives an embarrassed little cough and then delivers the second piece of news in the space of five minutes that drives every bit of breath from my body.

'I'm sorry, madam, I can't help you I'm afraid,' she says.

'Mr Hogg doesn't work here any more. He left the company a fortnight ago.'

I need to sit down.

'What's up?' Angie eyes me with alarm as I sink to the ground.

'My dad doesn't work there any more.'

'Did you forget?' Tug looks at me as if I've got a screw loose.

'No, of course not! I don't get it.' I rub my forehead, trying to think clearly. 'He hasn't said anything about leaving his job. He still goes off to work every day.'

'Perhaps he's got the sack,' says Angie, then bites her lip, too late.

'Maybe he's got a new job,' suggests Tug diplomatically, but the damage is done.

'I haven't got time to think about this now,' I mutter, struggling to my feet.

'Where are you going?' asks Angie.

'I've got to find Mum.'

'Wait for me, I'm coming with you,' she says. 'Tug, cover for us, will you?'

'No problem,' says Tug, giving us a wave. 'Good luck!'

Actually, I haven't got a clue where I'm going. I don't know where Mum's been taken for a start.

'Ring 999,' suggests Angie. Now we're on a mission

she's enjoying this, I can tell. She loves a bit of drama. Not like me, I've had enough of it to last a lifetime.

'Don't be daft,' I snap. 'Let me think.' Angie looks a bit affronted but waits patiently while I work out what to do next. At last, I decide what to do.

'There's that big police station the other side of the park. I bet they've taken her there.'

'Let's go!' Angie darts off so fast it's hard to keep up with her. I follow her through the gates of the park: past the café where elderly ladies sit gossiping over cups of tea; down the track by the tennis courts where I used to have my lessons, boo-hoo; on past the playground where dogs sit patiently tethered to railings while mums swing toddlers to and fro and chat to their friends; and up by the pond where two little kids with their mum are feeding the ducks, while a man, just like my dad, sits reading a paper . . .

I slow down to a walk, my chest heaving, as Angie disappears through the trees. Then I come to a full stop.

It *is* my dad.

My heart misses a beat because for a minute I think he's with the woman and kids and my overactive imagination says, 'So that's his game! He's leading a double life, you hear about it all the time. He's got another wife and children.' And my next thought is, no wonder he didn't want another baby! But then my heart returns to normal because the woman shakes the bread bag full of crumbs into the pond and says, 'That's your lot. Come on then, you two, or we'll miss the bus,' and the kids run after her, past Dad who raises his head from his paper and watches them out of sight. And I watch him, a lonely figure on a park bench gazing at other people's happy families, until he turns back to his paper and catches my eye.

'Gabby?' he says in surprise. 'What are you doing here? Shouldn't you be at school?'

'Shouldn't you be at work?' I retaliate. I see my father's cheeks flush red for the first time in my life.

'Mum's been arrested,' I say, saving him the embarrassment of a reply and have the satisfaction of seeing his jaw drop by a metre.

'Shop-lifting apparently.' I sound oddly conversational, even to my own ears, but he believes me straight away.

'Good grief,' he mutters. 'Where is she?'

'I'm not sure. At the police station, I guess. I was just on my way there.'

'Where's Henry?'

My blood runs cold. I haven't given a thought to little Hen.

'I dunno.'

'Right,' he says, then rubs his face in his hands. 'Right then.' He takes a deep breath, puts his hands on his knees and stands up decisively, folding his newspaper into a neat square, as meticulous as ever, and placing it in his pocket. 'I'd better sort this out. You get yourself back to school and I'll go to the police station.'

'No, I'm coming with you!'

'Just do as you're told, Gabby,' he says wearily and I'm about to protest further when he adds, 'Someone will need to collect the boys after school. Can you do that for me? I don't know how long all this is going to take.'

Suddenly I have a horrible vision of my mother locked up in a police cell overnight and my mouth goes dry. And Henry? Where's Henry? I nod my head miserably.

'Good girl. Don't worry, it'll be fine. Now back to school.'

I watch him as he strides purposefully away, just as Angie comes back to find where I've got to.

'That's your dad!' she says, staring at him in surprise as he disappears into the distance.

'I know,' I say. 'He's going to the police station to get Mum.'

'Oh,' she says in disappointment, then covers up quickly. 'That's good.'

'Yes,' I say, doubtfully. 'It'll be all right now. Dad is going to sort it all out.'

I don't do as I'm told. I don't want to go back to school. I can't face the Gemstones and, actually, I want to be on my own so I can start to take everything in and try to make sense of it all. 'You go,' I urge Angie. 'I don't want you to get done for truanting.'

'Are you sure?' asks Angie, torn between the fear of getting into trouble and the desire to find out what's going on. Only it's not quite so exciting for her now we're not going to the police station. 'Will you be all right on your own?'

'Yeah, I'm fine! Anyway, I won't be on my own, I'm going round to my gran's.'

'All right then. Catch you later.' Angie gives me a hug and she's off like the wind, terrified of Mimi being called up to school. I give a wry smile and sink down on to the bench my father has just vacated. I've been mourning Angie's absence from my life for the past month and now

I can't wait to get rid of her. How ironic is that? But I need to think.

What's happened to Mum? She's scaring me to death. Shop-lifting, for goodness sake! It's so completely out of character. But what is *in* character nowadays? I don't know any more. She's been acting weird for ages, ever since the baby was born . . .

Little Hen. I gulp. He's all right, isn't he? She wouldn't . . . ? I push the thought from my mind and turn my attention to Dad instead.

What's going on there? Why is he sitting in the park reading the paper when he should be at work? Why has he given up his job when he's always going on about us not having enough money? Why didn't he tell us what he'd done?

I don't get any of it. My head's pounding with it all and none of it makes sense. Flipping parents! You think you know them, don't you? You think you know everything there is to know about their sad, boring little lives which you've always assumed would be totally meaningless without you to look after. I mean, *I'm* the teenager, I'm the one who's supposed to be causing *them* grief! I'd have thought they'd have reached the age where I could trust them!

Not so long ago I could have set the clock by what time my father went out in the morning and came home at night and I absolutely knew where he was in between. I could tell you what my mother was going to say even before she opened her mouth (and it was always embarrassing) and where she would be and what she would be doing at any particular moment of the week. They were ancient, annoying, over-anxious, pushy but completely, utterly predictable.

I have just discovered that my mother is a criminal and my father is an unemployed layabout.

I made it up about going to Gran's just to get rid of Angie but suddenly I realize I want to talk to her. Gran will be the one to allay my fears with a few sharp, sensible words. She's going to have to know sooner or later anyway about all that's been going on. It might as well be now.

When I knock at the door she does a double-take.

'Why aren't you at school?' she asks suspiciously.

'Don't ask,' I say, brushing past her. 'Where do I start?'

Inside, fortified by a steaming mug of Gran's builder's tea, I prepare to begin the story. As soon as I say, 'It's Mum,' I wish I hadn't.

'What's she done now?' groans Gran as if Mum's a tearaway with history and has just been served with another asbo. Actually, that's not funny. Adults *can* get asbos, can't they? What if Mum gets one for shop-lifting and has her name all over the papers? The Gemstones are going to love that! I'll never live it down.

'She's been arrested for shop-lifting!' I say crossly and wait for the tirade. Only it doesn't come. I sip my tea and take a peek at her over the rim of the mug.

She's crying.

'Oh Gran,' I say and set down my tea quickly and put my arms round her. 'Don't worry. She won't go to prison. They don't send you to jail for your first offence.' I don't know if this is true, but it sounds as if it might be.

Her hand comes up to pat my arm. 'Course she won't,' she whispers. 'Poor thing.'

I'm more shocked than if she's called for Mum to be hung, drawn and quartered. In fact, I was prepared for that. Gran's like Dad, from the 'eye for an eye' school of thought. 'What they need is a bit of discipline' is a favourite saying of hers; 'Bring back military service' is another. The last thing I expected was a bit of compassion.

'Poor thing,' she repeats. 'She must be in such a state.'

I think of the stuff Gran doesn't know about: Mum not being able to sleep at night then dozing all day; Mum being irritable and exhausted all the time; Mum not bothering to get dressed until Dad comes home; Mum shutting the baby in the bedroom and ignoring his cries while she sits glued to the television; Mum screaming at Freddie, force-feeding him; Mum hurling the lemonade decanter at the wall and howling in distress.

'She is,' I admit.

'She's a good mother!' says Gran fiercely.

'I know she is.' And at that moment I realize it's true.

'She just can't cope at the moment.'

'That's right.'

We sit there, heads together, me with my arms round Gran, her patting my arm, thinking about Mum.

'It's all too much for her,' she says.

'I know.'

She's silent for a while. Then she says, 'I was like that.'

I sit up in surprise. 'Were you?'

She nods. 'I went to pieces when I had your mum. I thought I was going mad.'

'Really? But you only had one.'

'I know, that's why. I couldn't go through all that again.'

'What happened?'

'I couldn't sleep, I couldn't eat. I cried all the time. I just fell apart.'

'Oh Gran.'

'Everyone else managed. Why couldn't I? I felt a failure as a mother.' Her face is creased with distress.

'Poor thing.' My down-to-earth, competent, formidable Grandma, unable to cope. It's hard to believe.

'Looking back, she was such a good little thing. But her crying drove me mad. I wanted to drown her.'

I freeze.

'I wouldn't have.' She shakes her head. 'But I wanted to. Just to stop her crying, that's all. Just to stop her crying all the time.'

'Gran?' My voice sounds small.

'Yes?'

'Do you think Henry's all right?'

'Yes, of course he is.' She sits upright and holds me by the shoulders, looking straight into my eyes. 'Listen to me, Gabby. Your mother would never hurt that baby. She's just frightened that she might.'

Gran and I pick up the boys from school and make them egg and chips. Gran buys a strawberry gateau for dessert.

'Ummm, shop-bought,' drools Freddie, his mouth full of synthetic cream. He thinks it's a treat.

'Where's Mum and Dad?' asks Felix.

'They've had to go out,' I say. 'They'll be back soon.'

Felix looks at me enquiringly but Gran shakes her head. She's right. Time for explanations later.

Dad comes home with Mum after tea. She's pale but composed. Dad is carrying Henry, pressed tight to his shoulder. Gran and I exchange a look of relief.

Freddie is tired so Gran says she'll run a bath for him and he goes upstairs without a murmur. Before long she's back down again.

'That was quick,' says Mum. She's sipping a cup of tea Dad's made her and the colour is slowly returning to her cheeks.

Gran nods. 'He asked for a story but I told him I didn't have my glasses so I'd have to tell him one instead. I started to tell him all about my childhood. I must have bored him to tears, he was asleep in five minutes.'

We all laugh, though I know it's not true. I've learnt to my cost that, actually, grown-ups are seldom as boring as they seem. I've also learnt that since Mum has stopped fussing over him, Freddie goes down to sleep much easier.

'Do you want something to eat, Pauline?' asks Gran.

Mum shakes her head.

'What about you, Leonard?' persists Gran. 'You must be hungry, you've been at work all day.'

Dad looks at me and sighs. 'Actually, you'd all better sit down. There is something I need to tell you.'

We stay up late that night except for Freddie who's already in bed and probably doesn't need to know all that's been going on in this weird family of ours.

First of all Dad tells us he's lost his job, which, of course, I'd already worked out for myself. I think he must have told Mum down at the police station because she doesn't look surprised. He tells us how he was called into the office that day a few weeks ago by Mr Babcock and was given the news.

'Why did you keep it a secret?' Felix asks. 'You

always say we should tell the truth.'

'I didn't intend to,' he says, looking abashed. 'But your mother had her hands full with the new baby and I didn't want to worry her, so I left the house every day as if I was going to work. I just pretended for the time being that it hadn't happened and tried to carry on as if everything was normal.'

Felix nods understandingly. 'I do that too when I'm worried about something.'

'Do you?' Dad looks at him sympathetically.

'You must have been worried sick,' says Gran quietly.

He shrugs. 'In some ways it made life easier. It had been on the cards for a while.' He looks up at us all. 'I don't think I'd been doing the job well for some time. Getting too old, I suppose. It had been noted. When the baby was born it became even more difficult. I knew it was just a question of time before they gave me my marching orders. To be honest, it was a relief when they came at last.'

'But you must be concerned about money,' says Gran. 'Poor Leonard.'

'Does this mean I don't have to go to boarding school?' asks Felix eagerly.

Dad smiles. 'No, you're safe there, son. They were quite good actually, old Babcock and Brown. They came up trumps in the end and gave me a reasonably generous redundancy payment. Reward for all those years of service I suppose. Anyway, we're not going to starve, that's for sure, and there should be enough left over to put you through school.'

Felix's face falls. 'I don't want to go,' he says mutinously.

'Of course you do,' says Dad jovially, though his eyes are full of concern. 'It's my old school you know, you'll have a great time!'

'Listen to him, Dad!' I say. 'He's trying to tell you as clearly as he can, he doesn't want to go, but you won't listen.'

'Yes, Leonard, listen to him.' Mum speaks quietly but firmly. 'We talked about this down at the police station; that counsellor woman said we've got to stop pretending and learn to listen to each other.'

'Why were you at the police station?' asks Felix, puzzled.

Mum darts a look at Dad who nods. 'I was arrested for shop-lifting.'

'What?' Felix's face is a picture.

'I didn't know what I was doing,' explains Mum, looking sad. 'I was confused, upset. The baby wouldn't stop crying. And I was so, so tired, I just wanted to go to sleep. I was in the department store in the precinct and I forgot what I was in there for. I couldn't think straight. I just wanted to go home and get to bed.'

'Apparently I put some stuff in my bag and made for the door. I didn't even know what it was until they showed me. It was nothing I wanted. Little skinny tops and skirts, nothing that would fit me. I must have been thinking of you, Gabby. They've got a zero tolerance policy on shop-lifting in that store. Next thing I knew Henry and I were being whisked off to the police station.'

I get up and give her a hug, squeezing her tight. 'Poor Mum. Were they horrible to you?'

'No. They were very good down there, especially when they realized how young Henry was.' She turns to Gran. 'They haven't charged me, Mum. Apparently they think I'm suffering from post-natal depression. It's nothing to be ashamed of. They sent for a counsellor to talk to me. I was with her for ages. I'm going to see her again. It's very common.'

'I know,' says Gran.

When Angie comes to see Baby Hen at last, predictably she goes into raptures.

'He's gorgeous!' she gushes, rocking him so rapidly he looks alarmed.

'Is he?' I look at him objectively. I suppose he is improving every day. Now his eyes are open more, he reminds me of one of those little marmoset monkeys. He looks like an animal now instead of a vegetable.

'Of course he is! He's beautiful! And he's got teeny-weeny little fingers and he's got teeny-weeny little toes . . .' She strokes his hand then raises it to her lips and starts to kiss each tiny finger. A look of panic flits across Henry's features; he's not used to this much attention. 'I could eat him up, piece by piece,' she drools. Understandably, Henry's face puckers up and he starts to cry.

'Give him here!' I sigh and take him off her. 'He

doesn't like being fussed, do you, Hen? You like a quiet life.' I put him upright so he can see over my shoulder and he stops crying. 'There, that's better, isn't it?'

Angie looks on admiringly. 'You're so good with babies, Gabby.'

'No, I'm not. I don't even like them,' I say automatically.

Gran comes into the kitchen and chuckles. 'You could have fooled me.'

The kitchen smells delicious from the Caribbean vegetable soup, packed with pumpkins, yams and sweet potato, we've just had for lunch, courtesy of Mimi, of course. The table is littered with blue, baby boy wrapping paper. Angie's family has brought presents for the baby: a tiny set of velvety jacket, top and leggings from her mum; a soft, hand-knitted shawl from Mimi; a discarded, no-longer-loved, woolly rabbit from Talitha that had seen better days and, from Bolton, a tube of Smarties, immediately commandeered by Freddie on the justifiable grounds that, 'Henry can't eat them, he's got no teeth.' Fair enough.

'Share them with the others, Freddie!' Mum says. He frowns and I think he's going to make a fuss, but then he sits down and he counts them out meticulously, 'One for Talitha, one for Bolton, one for me . . .' A few weeks ago, he would have screamed blue murder and kept them all for himself. I notice he hangs on to all the red ones though. Still, it's progress.

They've gone now, having inspected Henry and pronounced him perfect.

Angie was so sheepish when she turned up first thing this morning with all her family in tow. Mimi was outraged that she hadn't told her the baby had been born and brought everybody round to see him immediately.

'Seems they had a row over some boy!' she says, holding Henry in the crook of her arm while she sways to and fro round our kitchen. Henry closes his eyes with pleasure and drifts off to sleep. 'I told her straight, Mrs Sheraton-Hogg, you don't fall out with your best friend over no boy!' Her voice rises in emphasis. 'Men!' she declares loudly. 'They're not worth it!'

Dad, who I catch sight of on his way downstairs, changes his mind and creeps back up.

'But this little man,' Mimi's voice becomes soft and creamy, 'he's as good as gold, aren't you, my precious?'

'Oh, he has his moments,' says Mum.

Mimi nods in understanding. 'They all do, my darling. I took my Kelvin back to the hospital when he was one week old and asked them to keep him. That boy never stopped bawling!'

'Did you?' says Mum with interest. She and Mimi and Angie's mum settle down for a big chinwag about babies, while Freddie, Talitha and Bolton play sliding down the stairs, and Henry sleeps on, his nose buried blissfully in Mimi's armpit. When they get up to go at last, Mum looks genuinely sorry and asks them to come again.

'We will, honey,' says Mimi, giving her a big hug. 'And if you want a night out with that husband of yours sometime, you just call Mimi. I'll baby-sit for you.' She looks around. 'Where is he, anyway?'

As soon as the door shuts behind them, Dad emerges from upstairs. 'Have they gone?' he whispers. 'Oh, sorry, Angie!' Angie giggles. He makes himself a cup of coffee and sits down beside us.

Mum seems loads better already. She's been seeing or talking to the counsellor on the phone every day and it seems to be doing the trick. Gran pops in every afternoon to give her a break and that helps too.

She's found a website as well and she's been talking to mums online who've been going through the same stuff. She's on it now on Dad's laptop. She thinks it's amazing.

'I don't feel so alone any more,' she says, scrolling through the messages. 'Other people feel like this as well. Look at this, Mum. This poor woman here hasn't managed to leave the house for a week. I thought it was just me.'

Gran goes over and reads the words on the screen, her

hands on Mum's shoulders. 'Poor soul,' she says. 'Tell her it'll get better.' Mum starts typing.

Felix comes in with his drawing pad and pencils and sits down at the table. 'What shall I draw?' he asks.

'Me!' squeals Angie and strikes a pose, so Felix obliges, sketching her quickly with bold, confident strokes.

'Let me see!' says Angie, impatient as ever. 'Felix! My nose looks really big!'

'No, it's you all right,' says Dad admiringly. 'That's very good, Felix.'

'My nose isn't that big!' protests Angie.

'OK, I'll make it smaller,' says Felix obligingly, making a more flattering profile with a few quick strokes. 'How's that?'

'Better,' says Angie with satisfaction. 'Can I keep it?'

'Sure.' Felix tears the page out, signs it with a flourish and presents it to Angie.

'You're very talented, son,' says Dad. 'I didn't realize quite how good you are. You could go far.'

Felix looks pleased. 'Do you want me to do you?'

Oh no! I've seen Felix's pictures of Dad. Not a good idea.

Dad looks surprised. 'All right then.'

Felix sketches, his brow furrowed with concentration. After a while I say, casually, 'My school has just got a new status, Dad.'

'Has it?'

'Keep still,' says Felix sternly.

'Sorry.'

'It's become a specialist art school,' I remark. 'I've got a letter about it in my bag. They're going to have a brand-new art department with a whole new suite of rooms and specialist teachers. It's going to be the best in the county.'

'Really?' says Dad.

'It'll be perfect for Felix then, won't it?' says Gran, turning away from the computer and joining us at the table.

'Can I go?' Felix puts down his pencil and paper and turns to Dad, his face alive with pleading. 'Please, Dad?' Mum gets up from the computer and sits down beside us.

Dad looks from one to the other. 'What about boarding school?'

'He doesn't want to go, Leonard,' says Mum, quietly.

'But it will be good for him,' says Dad. 'It'll make a man of him . . .'

'He'll be a man anyway. A man of his own making,' says Gran. 'Let the boy be.'

Dad looks at Felix. 'You really want to go to Gabby's school?'

Felix nods silently.

'You might get bullied, son.' Dad's voice goes down to a whisper. 'I was, you know.'

Felix contemplates him for a moment. 'I don't mind,' he whispers back.

Dad nods. 'I only ever wanted the best for you,' he says. His eyes sweep round the table. 'For all of you,' he adds. Mum picks up his hand and knits her fingers through his. I feel a lump in my throat.

'Anyone bullies Felix and they'll have our Kelvin to answer to,' says Angie staunchly. 'He's in the sixth form next year, he'll be a prefect.'

'And Tug,' I say quickly. 'Tug will keep an eye on you, Fee.'

'Who's Tug?' asks Mum. 'Is that the boy you fell out over?'

'No way!' we say in unison.

'Tug is Gabby's boyfriend,' grins Angie.

Dad looks alarmed.

'No he's not, he's my tennis partner!'

Angie snorts. 'He only plays so he can be near you.'

'That is so not true!' I protest, but I feel a warm glow of happiness spreading inside me.

'Thanks,' says Felix. 'But I don't need anyone to keep an eye on me. I can manage.'

Dad picks up the picture of himself and studies it for a long time. I hold my breath then risk a peek over his shoulder.

It's OK. It's not a picture of an evil king with great black boots. It's just a drawing of a balding, middle-aged guy with a long, mournful face, a droopy moustache and kind eyes.

It's Dad all right. Felix has got his measure.

Dad sighs and nods.

'Do you know,' he says, 'I think you can.'

32C, THAT'S ME

Chris Higgins

Who says you can't always get what you want?
You can if you have luck on your side.
I wanted to go out with the best-looking guy
in the school – and now I am.
I wanted the lead in the school play – and I
got it.
Life doesn't get better than that.

Until one day a simple phone message turns the
best day of your life into the worst . . . and
things won't ever be the same again.

PRIDE AND PENALTIES

Chris Higgins

'I rushed out of school clutching my letter. I couldn't wait to tell Dad my news.'

I only ever wanted my dad to be proud of me. So I'm a girl who wants to play rugby. What's wrong with that?

It's hard when your brother's constantly in the spotlight . . . but now he's got a secret of his own and so has Mum.

Being in this family is like being tangled up in a web – they don't call me Spider for nothing!

IT'S A 50/50 THING

Chris Higgins

With Mum on the verge of a breakdown and Dad not around anymore, Kally's new life is full of secrets.

When the gorgeous Jem skates into Kally's life and sweeps her off her feet, things finally seem to be going right.

But as Jem teaches her new tricks, Kally discovers there's more than one side to him and soon her life is spinning out of control . . .

A PERFECT TEN

Chris Higgins

Eva wants to be the best, just like her sister, Amber. Now she's queen of the gymnastics club, the girl everyone envies. Her life seems perfect.

But her hard work comes at a price. When new girl Patty joins the club, Eva's plans start to unravel and secrets that have long been hidden threaten to surface . . .

WOULD YOU RATHER?

Chris Higgins

Life is all about choices.

Daddy or chips? Boyfriend or career? Snog or marry? is the game that Flick and her friends love to play. But when her dad uncovers a long lost secret that unveils a mystery at the heart of her family, Flick discovers that not all choices are a game.

Some decisions can affect the lives of those around you for many *many* years to come . . .